IN THE SHADOW OF MALICE

NANCY C. WEEKS

author of *In the Shadow of Greed*

and *In the Shadow of Evil*

Mary,
Puch a joy to meet
you,
hugs!
Nancy C. Weeks

CRIMSON
ROMANCE

F+W Media, Inc.

Published by
Crimson Romance
an imprint of F+W Media, Inc.
10151 Carver Road, Suite 200
Blue Ash, OH 45242. U.S.A.
www.crimsonromance.com

ISBN 10: 1-4405-8028-6
ISBN 13: 978-1-4405-8028-4
eISBN 10: 1-4405-8029-4
eISBN 13: 978-1-4405-8029-1

Cover art © iStockphoto.com/CarolMRobinson; pxhidalgo/123RF

Chapter One

Almost midnight, an empty parking lot, no prying eyes.

Adam Blake hit the key fob, locking his sedan as he stepped out of the shadows. His senses picked up a hint of the wild honeysuckle that grew along the chain-linked fence lining the west side of Pete's Diner. As a warm May breeze washed over him, he rolled the tension from his shoulders and scanned the perimeter. Nothing appeared out of the ordinary.

Quite frankly, the reason he kept coming back surprised the hell out of him. Even though the food was great, Adam craved the company the small diner provided. The regulars were all so damn normal. Adam needed normal.

His life had become a reflection of what he did for a living and he needed a drastic change. Pete's Diner had become a baby step in that direction. The occasional hour spent with familiar strangers chased away his lonely, harsh existence.

From his position, he could identify the two people who remained in the deserted restaurant. The wizened old trucker was there on his weekly run from Norfolk, Virginia, to New Haven, Connecticut. The young woman sitting alone in one of the booths was the owner's granddaughter. From what Adam could surmise, Calista Martin had no life outside the diner other than her music studies at the university a few miles down the road. The ever-present cello case propped on the bench next to her kept her company.

The double doors behind the counter opened and a big man in a navy blue double-breasted chef's coat and sculled cap set a large silverware caddy on the counter. Pete Bradshaw was built like a guerrilla on steroids. Strands of blond-gray hair escaped the edges of his cap and gray stubble covered his chin. But what stood out most was the enormous fried egg skull tattoo on his left arm, the yellow yolk resting right in the center of the left eye socket.

Calista approached Pete as he poured coffee into a travel mug. The hard angles of his face softened when he glanced at her. He replaced the carafe back on the heating unit and a grin spread across his face. A bellowed cheer loud enough to rattle the windows followed as he lifted her into his arms and swung her around like she was a little girl. She wrapped her arms around his shoulders and gave him a quick hug before turning to the trucker and hugging him as well.

The celebratory moment could only mean one thing: Calista Martin posted her final assignment for her master's degree in music performance and secondary education. The bright smile on her face sent an unusual feeling of warmth into the pit of Adam's stomach. For reasons he was too tired to define, a sense of pride for her accomplishments raced through him. He recognized the strength and dedication it took for Calista to follow her dream. Adam had no dreams other than to protect those he loved and to stay alive one more day.

Her beaming smile pulled at Adam like a magnet, forcing his feet to step closer to the entrance. Removing her arms from around the older man's shoulder, she paused and turned toward the window. Their eyes held before she raised her hand and motioned for him to come inside. She moved toward the door and held it open for him.

"Am I too late for a quick burger?" Adam asked, closing the door behind him.

"The kitchen is still open. Pete will make you something."

Calista lowered her eyes and eased away from him. A hint of pink came into her cheeks. She acted the same jitterish way every time he got too close. Most people gave him a wide berth and that was usually fine with him. But Calista was so open and friendly to everyone who came through the door. For some reason, it pissed him off that she treated him with the same wariness everyone else did. He wanted that normal symbol of kindness she gave to others too, at least here.

The trucker set his ticket and a twenty down by the register. "Calista. Heading out."

She stepped out of the path of the doorway. "Thanks, Nate. Be careful on the road tonight."

"Always. And you get out of this grease-hole. Celebrate." He placed a Nationals baseball cap on his head. "Yo, Pete. Where's my jitter juice?"

"Watch your mouth, or the owner of this grease-hole may just spit in your next meatloaf."

Pete's voice was low, menacing, but his jovial expression gave away his true nature. He took the travel cup, waited a second for the last drip of fresh brewed coffee to drop into the carafe, and filled the oversized mug.

The scent of fresh, hot coffee wafted across the room, masking the overpowering odor of greasy fries. Adam inhaled, hoping the scent of caffeine would revive him. Pete took a cup from beneath the counter, filled it to the brim, and set it at Adam's regular table.

"Same-old-same-old tonight, Adam?"

Adam took a deep sip of the hot brew. "That would be great, but make it to go. If I sit here for too long, I'll be out for the night."

"No problem. It will be right out," he said before facing his granddaughter. Calista busied herself with wrapping silverware into napkins and then placing them in the caddy next to the menus. Pete took out another cup, filled it half full, and set it next to her.

"I can't drink coffee this time of night," she murmured at her grandfather like he should know better than to tempt her.

"Half a cup isn't going to kill you." A smirky grin appeared on his face. "Neither would a good roll … "

"Pete! God, the things that come out of your mouth." Calista picked up the mug and brought it to her nose, taking in the scent of the strong, rich brew. "And you can't joke about spitting in people's food." She took a sip, closed her eyes and swallowed. A groan of pure pleasure rumbled in her throat.

Adam coughed out his coffee and almost swallowed his tongue. Calista Martin was a walking, talking sensual magnet if ever there was one. From her shoulder-length strawberry blond curls that bounced when she moved to those warm cocoa, almond eyes that made a man feel noticed, Calista was a natural beauty with a body that would give a blind man wet dreams. Her groan sent blood rushing to dormant places better left alone.

To hide the growl that slipped through his lips, he chortled. Calista gave him a hard glare but again quickly lowered her eyes. Pete let out another window-rattling laugh, which sent Calista's cheeks and neck into a deep crimson glow. Before he returned through the swinging doors to the kitchen, he nudged her and said, "Tell Adam your news."

"What news, Calista?"

"It's nothing really. I just turned in my last assignment for my master's degree."

Adam rose, and lifting his coffee mug, tapped her mug lightly on the rim. "Congratulations. That's fantastic." He eased back into the booth. "So, what's next for you?"

"After six years and 166 college credits, the only thing in my near future is uninterrupted sleep."

Adam let out a chuckle. "Will you teach or perform?"

"Both. I have sent several audition tapes to orchestras and applied to just as many teaching positions. Now I have to see who bites. The best scenario is I'm hired to perform where I can also teach."

When she lifted her eyes to meet his gaze, her mouth opened to say something, but all she produced was a noisy breath. She darted off her stool and pointed to the corner of his right eye. "You're bleeding."

Adam yanked a couple napkins from the dispenser and blotted the area around the small Band-Aid. A couple drops of blood must have pooled at the corner of the bandage and dripped down the side of his face. He gave the area a quick wipe, crumbled the napkin, and placed it in his pocket.

"What happened?"

"It's nothing. Work accident. A protester didn't like the guy I was protecting. Threw a bottle at him but hit me instead. I should have grabbed a larger Band-Aid."

"I don't think it's nothing." She lifted his hair away from the area. "Have you seen it? The skin is turning a nasty shade of black and blue."

Calista moved behind the counter and pulled out a first-aid kit. She approached the table, cupped his jaw in her hand, and gently peeled off the Band-Aid. The feel of her hand on his face sent an unexpected jolt through him. He shifted his face out of her reach. "It's nothing."

Ripping open the gauze package, she folded it in half, and laid it on the wound, applying pressure. Something sharp slid over the cut, making him cringe.

"Damn, that's not helping, Calista."

She removed the gauze. A small, brownish piece of glass was mixed in with the blood. "Pete said you run a security firm. Maybe you need to ask for combat pay."

"Can't ask for more pay if it's your own company. I practically work for free so I can give my employees combat pay." He then eased her hand away from his head, holding down the bandage himself. "Don't fuss. It's no big deal."

"You could have a concussion, Adam."

"I don't." He grabbed another swatch of gauze from the kit and ripped it open. He added a squeeze of antibiotic ointment, and attached it with tape to his forehead. "See, all better."

Calista gave him a hard stare before she closed the first-aid kit and replaced it behind the counter. She picked up a spray bottle of cleaner and began to spray down the counter. "It's your noggin."

Pete came back through the kitchen door and set a to-go container down next to Adam before he addressed his granddaughter. "Put that rag down, Calista. You're not closing tonight. Pack up and get out of here."

"You let the other waitress go home. I'm all you've got. Besides, we shared a ride."

"Believe it or not, I can manage without you. And the night my granddaughter earns her master's degree, she doesn't close down this grease trap. Take the car. I'll catch a bus or walk home."

Calista placed her hands on her hips. "I'm not leaving you to close by yourself and walk home. How are you going to go by and visit Mimi if you don't have a car? I'll take the bus."

Adam stood. "I can give Calista a ride home." He reached into his coat pocket for his wallet. Placing a twenty down next to the register like the last customer, he grabbed his to-go bag and leaned his shoulder against the door. "Calista, "I'm ready whenever you are."

Calista busied herself by stuffing her laptop into her canvas bag, her fingers fidgeting with the zipper. As Adam waited for some sort of acknowledgment, he pushed down the irritation forming in the pit of his stomach. Even when he was trying to be a good guy, do a normal guy kind of thing, he was still treated like an asshole.

"It's just a ride home, Calista. I'm too scared of your grandfather to try anything."

"You don't have to do that. The bus stop is right there," she said, pointing toward the parking lot.

"I know where the bus stop is." Adam reached for her large case and paused by the door.

She stood still, studying him until he almost fidgeted. "I don't accept rides from anyone unless I know their last name."

8

"Blake. Adam Blake."

Calista first glanced at her grandfather. He gave her a nod. The room grew quiet while she made up her mind. She finally shrugged and said, "I would love a ride home. Lead the way." She reached up and gave Pete a kiss on his cheek. "Give Mimi my love."

"Your grandmother will be so proud of you. I can't wait to tell her ..."

He stopped as if his words clogged his throat.

"It's okay, Pete. Mimi's heart knows, her soul knows, and you're right. She's very proud of me." Calista wiped away the tear that threatened to spill down her grandfather's cheek. With another quick hug, she walked out to the parking lot.

Adam moved ahead of her, positioning his body so it shielded her between him and the building. A soft crunch near the dumpster sounded behind him. He froze. With his arms tight against his body, the familiar rush of adrenaline filled his veins. He shifted his position toward the dark shadows. A large calico cat bounced off the structure and disappeared into the bushes.

"That's Max. He and Pete have an understanding."

"It's a cat. How do you have an understanding with a cat?"

"He brings Pete dead mice and Pete makes sure Max eats like a king."

Adam chuckled. Something he seemed to do a lot around Calista. With one final visual sweep, he relaxed his stance and opened the passenger door of his Acura. After Calista was settled in the deep leather seat, he ambled around and unlocked the trunk, placing her cello in the bay. He slammed the trunk and got behind the wheel.

Before he could stop himself, he asked the question that had been bugging him. "I thought I heard your grandmother passed away a while back. Did I misunderstand?"

"No, you heard right."

"But you just told Pete to …"

"He drives to the cemetery every night after he closes the diner, sits next to her gravestone, and tells her about his day. They were married fifty years. That isn't a loss you ever get over."

"And your parents? They are gone too?"

"Yes, it's just Pete and me. Mom and Dad died in a car accident when I was eleven. Mimi and Pete raised me." Calista twisted so she would face him. "What about you?"

"The same. Both parents gone."

Adam hadn't a clue why he brought the subject up. He had no business spending time with Calista outside the diner. That wasn't a baby step into a normal existence, but a giant leap off a high cliff. His life made him hell on relationships.

But there was just something about Calista he couldn't ignore. Maybe it was time to see if there was anything between them. If not, he could just walk away before he hurt her, too.

"I'm sorry about your parents." She placed a hand over his arm. Their gazes held before she broke away and scanned the interior of his car. "I figured you would drive some sporty number or one of those black, mysterious SUVs."

"What's a black, mysterious SUV?"

"You know. One of those cool bulletproof numbers with blacked out windows."

"Calista, just what do you think I do?"

"You're like Batman." Her voice was barely above a whisper and she squirmed in her seat, her gaze on a spot in her lap. "When you leave the diner, you return to your bat cave unless you're out fighting bad guys."

He grimaced. *Now what, smartass? Lie to her, or tell her who you really are and what you do?*

"Who knew music teachers had such active imaginations? I'm no superhero."

He could never tell her what he did for a living. His path may have been chosen for him, but he hadn't walked away when he had the chance.

"And I'm not a music teacher—yet."

"You're going to be hired so fast, your head will spin." He placed the key in the ignition and started the car. Backing out of the space, he pulled onto the side street.

"Where are you going?" Her voice sounded normal.

Adam slowed and stopped at the light. "I'm taking you home."

"But I didn't tell you where I live."

"Yeah, I guess I need that, don't I? This is the way the Metro bus always turns."

Calista grinned. "It's not far. Take the second left. My neighborhood is a couple miles on the other side of the beltway. Once you pass over I-495, I'll direct you."

Following her directions, Adam headed north on the deserted street. The faded streetlights casted a fluorescent gloom over homes on either side of the street, but the lack of lighting didn't distract from the well-cared neighborhood. People took pride in their homes much like the suburbs of Los Angeles, where he grew up. There was a time when someone like Calista was exactly the type of woman he dreamed of settling down with and raising a bunch of little Blakes. She had a kindness in her that he sorely missed. But with the twelve jaded, nightmarish years he had on her that he could never erase, that dream was gone. It couldn't exist in his reality now.

"What's wrong? You're so tense."

"Sorry, my mind was on something else."

"If you get on the Beltway here, you can get off at the next exit, avoiding all the lights."

Adam turned on his blinker and eased over a lane. Just as he entered the entrance ramp, a stabbing pain exploded in the back of his eyes, ricocheting across his frontal lobe. An involuntary, animalistic moan escaped through his clenched teeth and he squeezed his eyes shut against the searing pain. His hands shot up to cover his head as his foot slammed down on the accelerator. The car shot across the road, jumping the curb, and hurled up a slope. Adam hit the brake inches before the front bumper smashed into the trunk of an old oak tree. His forehead smashed into the horn, the blaring sound deafening.

"Adam?"

Calista slammed the gearshift in park and shut off the ignition. She pulled his head away from the steering wheel. "Adam, what's wrong?" She tried to remove his hands from his head, but he held on tight.

He couldn't think, couldn't reason. He swallowed the acidic bile in his throat. The blinding pain increased until he thought his head would burst. Then the sound of a child's desperate cry filled his head. *They're hurting Mommy! Help her!*

What the fuck was that? Every word of the child's plea seemed to cut through his frontal lobe to the back of his head. A gripping panic slammed into him as he fumbled in his jacket pockets. "My cell. Find my cell."

Calista searched his pockets. "Here, Adam. I'll call 911."

"No. No."

He dropped his head back against the seat. Everything around him faded in and out of focus—except Calista. The pain pounded between his ears as dark, red spotted dots swam over his vision, allowing only minimal light in. Sweat beaded around his eyes and screamed down his spine. He shook his head to clear his vision and grabbed the phone. It took a couple tries, but a line on the other end began to ring.

Calista gasped, her hands covering her mouth. "God, you're bleeding again, but not from the wound on your head. It's coming from your eyes." She swiped a finger at the corner of his eye and her fingers came away dripping with his blood. "I need to get you to a hospital."

He began to shake his head, but the pain was so bad, he froze. The phone continued to ring in his ear. Eighth ring, ninth. On the tenth ring, it was picked up.

"Rina." His best friend's name came out in a raspy whisper. "Rina."

"Katrina is a little busy right now, Blake. Why don't you join the party?"

The man's voice came out in a thick, rough, eastern European accent. Adam recognized it and a chill spiked through him.

The agony in the scream he heard next pierced Adam's heart. He shoved down the sharp pain in his head and allowed the years of training to resurface.

"You're dead, Ludis. You hear me. Your fucking life is over," he ground out.

"Big words. I'm going to carve her open then hunt down the kid. Your kid, you motherfucker. And when I'm done with her, I'm coming for you."

The line went dead.

Chapter Two

Calista placed her hand on Adam's shoulder. His muscles trembled beneath her touch, sending a pulse of grief right to her heart. She caressed his shoulder then pressed her hand against his hand, which still clutched his phone to his ear. Adam's tortured gaze met hers and he jerked her hand away, shoving the phone back in his sports coat.

He pressed his temples with his fingertips and said, "Get out of the car, Calista."

"No. I'm not leaving you. You need a doctor."

Her voice sounded calm to her own ears, but everything in her wanted to run. Tidbits of Adam's conversation with a man named Ludis mixed with Calista's nightmarish visions of her best friend's screams; Hanna's blood smeared over the walls and matted in her hair, the agony from the monster's knife so excruciating, Hanna's mind slipped into the darkest hell, never to open again. They buried her on a cold, dreary day, a fitting scene for such a horrific loss.

Calista's eyes began to fill. She shut them, bit down on her bottom lip before drawing in a deep, cleansing breath. This wasn't the time to freak out. Blood mixed with tears streamed down the side of Adam's face. Air, maybe he needed air. She turned the key and hit the button on the door. The window slid down, letting in the cool night breeze. With the sleeve of her blouse, she blotted the bleeding from the corner of his eye.

Was this an aneurysm? She knew next to nothing about medicine. But damn it, eyes didn't bleed.

"Get out, Calista. I have to go." Adam's voice grew weak, the last word was almost inaudible.

"You can't drive." She choked on the last word. Her heart pounded between her ears, drowning out the world around her.

Only Adam existed. She tried to remember her first aid lessons, but nothing she had ever learned covered this.

A moan escaped his lips. "It's better. The pain is lessening."

"Liar. Your face is as white as your shirt. I'll drive you."

"No! Hell, no."

"Damn it, Adam. Change seats with me and tell me the address."

"I can't get you involved."

His pain-filled voice squeezed her heart and she silently began to pray. *God, please don't let him die.*

She clutched his hands in hers. "I'm not leaving you."

Since Hanna's death, Calista had walked out of her own life, slamming the door to the reckless, fun-loving person of her past, and hid under the shield of her grandfather's diner for the last fifteen months. But that shield didn't protect her from the nightmares or guard her from the violence in the world she couldn't control. It found her anyway. As easy as it would be to open the door and step out of the car, she would never forgive herself for leaving Adam alone.

She yanked the keys from the ignition, got out of the car, and raced around to the driver's side. She threw open the door and tried to shove him over into the passenger seat.

"Move over."

"Give me the damn keys. Now." He tried to grab them, but she stepped out of his reach. He glared up at her. "You have no idea what you're getting yourself into. This can't touch *you*."

Calista nudged Adam with her hip, trying to force him out of the driver's seat. "I'm not leaving." She shoved one more time and he scooted over the console into the passenger seat. Part of her was elated she won the battle of wills. The other part was scared shitless.

"Address?"

"Take the Chevy Chase exit."

She started the car and backed down the embankment. Spinning the steering wheel, she sped out onto the short entrance. Once on the Beltway, she weaved through three lanes of traffic. The adrenaline pumping through her veins kept the fear in check, and she pressed down on the accelerator. The speedometer hit ninety.

"Slow down, Calista."

"No."

Thank God traffic was light. She slowed just long enough to take the Chevy Chase exit. "Who was that guy on the phone?" She didn't want to know, but she had to ask.

Adam rubbed his hand behind his neck, his eyes fixed on the highway. "No one. You're giving me a ride. That's it. Take the next left, and for God's sake, slow the hell down."

Calista spun around the neighborhood street so fast she gripped the steering wheel to keep her shoulder from slamming into the door. Her speed dropped to fifty. From the corner of her eye, she could see the color in Adam's face return.

"How's the pain in your head?"

"Almost gone. Take the next right."

She slowed down and drove into an old, established neighborhood. She glanced at Adam. Another blood-soaked tear streamed down the side of his face. He lifted his hand and swiped at it, leaving a smear near his hairline. "Adam? What happened back on the entrance ramp?"

"I don't know." His voice came out in a forced whisper and he cleared his throat. "I got this excruciating pain behind my eyes and then … "

"Maybe it's from the wound on your forehead. You need an ER."

"It's not. Next right," he said, pointing to the upcoming street.

Calista swallowed a lump in her throat the size of a golf ball. "I heard the man on the other end of the call. He said after he carves her open … "

She clamped her jaw tight to keep the sob at bay. If she allowed the dam of fear to open, she would be no use to anyone.

Adam rested his palm over her hand clamped on the steering wheel. "No questions, Calista. You're better off knowing nothing about any of this." He paused then said, "Just forget it ever happened."

"How?" Her stomach pitched as fear spiked down her spine.

He removed his hand and pressed her shoulder, the warmth easing away a little of the panic. "Pull over next to the large oak, two houses up on the right."

Calista maneuvered the car into a spot and turned off the engine. She twisted in her seat to face him. He reached behind him and pulled a black duffel bag from the back seat. He unzipped it and pulled out a gun. She couldn't take her eyes off the offensive weapon.

Pete made sure she knew how to handle a gun because he kept them in the house. He told her grandmother it would be safer if she learned how to use one than to hide it away under lock and key. But Calista always hated the weapons and wanted nothing to do with them.

The Glock seemed to fit Adam's hand perfectly, an extension of himself. Her heart drummed so loudly in her chest, she was surprised the sound didn't vibrate off the car's interior walls. "What do I do? How can I help?"

"You can't help, Calista. As soon as I get out of this car, you're going to drive away. Understand?" His hand clamped down hard on her hands intertwined in her lap. "Look at me."

Calista met his glare. "I can help. Pete has a Glock and taught me how to use it. I don't understand what's going on, but you're not one hundred percent. You can't go into that house the way you are. Let me help."

"No." He unbuckled his seat belt, switched off the overhead lights on the dash and opened the door. "Get the hell out of here.

Now." His dark eyes seemed to burrow right into her heart. "Sorry about all of this. It was just supposed to be a normal ride home."

"Adam, wait," she whispered, but he shut the door, cutting off her reply. He placed the Glock in the waistband against his back and darted behind the car. Calista followed his progress across the street. He disappeared behind the side of the house two doors up.

Everything was eerily silent. It was as if all the nightlife knew what was happening behind closed doors. Calista's gaze darted up and down the street. The few cars parked on the curb were empty. She should leave just like Adam commanded, but she couldn't. He needed her. She felt it in her bones.

There was only one other time in her life that she'd felt the same gut-wrenching pull to stay put: the day she abandoned Hanna to her fate, too eager for a weekend trip to wait for her friend. That feeling she ignored and she would pay for that mistake for the rest of her life. Standing at her best friend's gravesite, she'd made a vow. No matter how scared, she would never turn her back on a friend again. She didn't have a clue who Adam Blake really was, but the Adam from the diner was a friend.

"This is restitution for Hanna," she whispered in the empty car. Before she could talk herself out of probably the stupidest thing she ever did in her twenty-five years, she opened the door and got out.

Damn, where the hell are the crickets, frogs, fireflies? What do they know I don't?

She crept up against the large oak and glanced around it. Using the long shadow of the tree, she sprinted in front of the first house. No lights illuminated the lawn. She then ran across the driveway into the front lawn of the next house.

Staying in the shadows, she crossed into the yard, making her way onto the porch. Just as she gripped the doorknob, a large crash sounded from inside followed by a loud groan. She hopped down off the porch and crunched behind a large crape myrtle.

Seconds later, the front door smashed open, banging against the wall, and a man raced from the house. Calista curled into a tight ball and froze. He held his shoulder, blood oozing between his fingers. She didn't breathe, didn't move an inch, but she couldn't help memorizing the man's every feature: tall, slim frame; square jaw; and long, straight, white-blonde hair. He fled down the steps onto the curved sidewalk and jogged across the grass. Calista ducked further behind the bush. She watched as he scanned the porch before getting in his car. He sped away down the street before he even closed the door.

Calista inched out of her hiding place. Every nerve screamed to bolt, but her feet edged closer to the door. Her grandfather's words echoed in her head. *Face fear and it will disappear. Avoid it, fear will swallow you whole.*

She was so damn tired of being afraid. She peered around the doorway into the foyer as her heart crashed against her ribcage. The foyer opened to a family room where Adam sat on the floor with a woman covered in blood in his arms.

"Is she...dead?"

• • •

"Damn it, Calista. I told you to get the hell out of here." Fury sliced through him as his gaze darted behind Calista. Did Ludis see her? The thought terrified him. He was in no position to protect her.

"The man who just left, did you see him?"

"Yes, but he's gone."

His gaze returned to the woman in his arms and he gulped in air. The truth swelled the passageway to his lungs as tightly as his clenched fist. Rina's blood pulsed against the skin of his palm. No matter how hard he applied pressure, she was losing blood at an alarming rate.

"What can I do?"

"Hand me the small sweater on the clothes tree."

Calista grabbed the piece of clothing and knelt down next to him. He scrunched it into a ball and pressed it against Rina's chest wound.

It took him only seconds to disarm the two men with Ludis. When he lunged toward Ludis, the bastard panicked. He pierced his knife through Rina's chest, tossing her body against Adam. The wound was too deep. Nothing he did would matter, but he had to try.

"I'm calling an ambulance."

"Put the phone down, Calista."

"Adam? Damn it, you can't help her."

"I know. No one can."

She sucked in a sharp breath. Her shocked features glared at him then scanned the room, settling on the two dead men, one sprawled across the Oriental rug, his neck twisted in an odd angle, the second slumped over the sofa with two large knifes wedged into his abdomen and chest.

He broke eye contact with Calista and glanced down at his friend. White, searing anger raged through him. His chest heaved with lack of oxygen as his heart hammered.

"Adam." The faint whisper filled him.

"Rina. God, hang on." He brushed the hair from her face and lifted her closer so he could hear her.

"Ludis ... he knows." She swallowed the pain and tried again. "They know."

"Shhh, don't try to talk ... "

"No. Listen. Vasnev knows—"

"Knows what? Rina? "

She touched his face with her blood-covered fingers. He swallowed a sob that threatened to choke him.

"Everything."

Adam shook his head. "No, that's not possible." A fist clamped down on his heart and squeezed. How could Vasnev know they lived, that Anna existed?

The moment they had discovered Rina was pregnant, Adam planned their deaths so carefully. Rina's car was witnessed going off a cliff in the Brenner Pass. His taped execution by a radical group in a hole in Afghanistan was perfectly implemented. Hell, Adam's passing was still talked about in the halls of the CIA six years later.

He swiped a strand of matted hair from her cheek. "We were careful."

"Anna. Promise—she needs you. Keep her safe."

Rina's eyes closed.

"Rina, stay with me." He patted her bruised cheek until she opened her eyes. "I can't do it alone."

"Promise. Anna. Promise."

"God, of course."

Her gaze locked on his as her hand caressed his cheek then fell to her side as if it weighed a ton. With a slight nod of her head, her body trembled, and went limp in his arms.

"Rina. Damn it, Rina. Don't you dare leave me." Adam gently lowered her to the floor and began chest compressions. "Anna needs you. I need you."

The blood gushed out the long gashes in her abdomen with each compression.

She can't be gone.

The air shifted and he glanced at Calista. She had knelt down next to him and wrapped her arm around his waist, resting her head against his back. With her other hand, she covered his hands. Rina's blood seeped through his fingers, staining her palm.

"She's gone, Adam," she said, her face wet with tears. "Who is Anna?"

"Rina's four-year-old daughter."

Calista placed a hand on his shoulder. "Where is she?"

Adam observed Calista's mouth move, but her words didn't register. The blood smeared over his palm did. An icy vengeance crept into his heart, keeping it beating. Ludis would pay. He would make him pay.

"Adam." Calista shook him hard. "Anna. Where's Anna?"

The desperation in her voice knocked him out of the trance. He stood abruptly and stepped back from Rina's body. Closing his eyes for only a moment, he focused on two unbeatable forces from within: the soldier and the father. When he opened his eyes, he knew what he had to do. He yanked out the tail of his shirt and wiped his hands. "In the panic room upstairs. Follow me, but don't touch anything. Understand?"

"Yes." She shot him a glare, then her eyes softened. "I understand."

At the staircase threshold, he stopped again. "I mean it, Calista. I don't want anyone to know you were here. Your name can't be linked with mine on a damn police report."

"But how ..."

"I can't explain." He swallowed hard. "But I will when you and Anna are safe."

The upstairs hallway had four doors. He opened the third door down and entered a child's room, glancing to Calista. "Remember, don't touch anything."

Moving over to the closet, he pushed the clothes away. On the shelf behind the books, he found the hidden metal panel that matched the bookshelves perfectly. He tapped the right corner and a small door popped open, revealing a touch pad. He punched in an eight-digit code and stepped back. The wall slipped away. A steel door stood in front of him with another keypad. This time, he punched in a code and an iris scanner popped out. Adam placed his eye in the circular disk. It took seconds for a thin light to swipe his eye before the door whooshed open.

He nearly stumbled in his haste to get into the spacious playroom. "Anna?"

His voice cracked. She wasn't there. Air left his lungs and his heart dropped to the pit of his stomach.

"Anna, baby girl, where are you?" He searched the hiding places behind the sofa and furnishings. He stopped in the middle of the room and listened. Calista stood silently in the doorway.

After a couple of seconds, a faint whimper came from the wardrobe against the back wall. Adam swung open the door and lifted the young girl curled into the fetal position into his arms. He dropped to the floor and rocked her back and forth. "Anna, talk to me. Are you hurt?"

Burning fear sliced through every nerve as his hand roamed over Anna's shoulder, arm, and leg searching for injuries. The hint of berries and vanilla from her shampoo mixed with the coppery stench of Rina's death. The two scents didn't belong in the same universe.

Anna had captured his cold heart seconds after she was born. It was his job to protect her. He wrapped Anna's trembling body tighter against his. How much did she see? Did anyone see her? The thought of Ludis's hands on Anna made Adam want to rip the man's liver out and make him eat it.

How in the hell was he going to tell this precious little girl about her mother?

He brushed her hair out of her face. "Anna. Look at me, baby."

Her arms circled his neck, clinging to him as if her life depended on it. Not a sound came from her lips, but she clung to him with such trust, as if he would fix everything, make her world normal again.

"I got you, Anna. Are you hurt?"

"No, but Mommy ... "

The words screamed inside his head. "I know, sweetheart." Her body shook as gut-wrenching sobs took control.

Adam could feel Calista behind him. Why the hell didn't she drive away like she promised? She was supposed to bring normal to his life, but instead, the horrors of his life were spread out on the living room floor, branding the scene in her mind forever.

A hand touched his shoulder. "Adam. We have to get her out of here."

Once again, his mind churned to order. He stood, wrapped Anna tightly against him, and turned to Calista. "I'm going to need your help."

"Just tell me what to do."

He wrapped his free hand around her neck and drew her close to him. Her body heat, her unexpected steadiness settled him as he impulsively pressed his lips to Calista's forehead, then released her.

He grabbed the red backpack out of a compartment above the door of the wardrobe and handed it to her. He then reached into the wardrobe for a worn stuffed elephant. "There's a quilt in the trunk," he said, pointing to the piece of furniture in front of the sofa.

When Calista reached for the lid, he caught her hand.

"Sorry. Touch nothing. Got it." She shrugged the pack over her shoulder and used her foot to open the lid. She pulled out the quilt. "What else does she need?"

He scanned the room. "The photo—next to the sofa."

The framed picture was of Anna with her arms wrapped around her mother's neck, both with huge smiles on their faces. The backdrop—the large ape house at the National Zoo. Adam couldn't be seen with them, but he watched them, took photos. The memory of that day sliced another deep hole into his heart as he tore open the back of the frame and removed the photo.

Calista picked up a Harry Potter book on the end table and slipped it inside her purse. "Now what?"

"Hand me the quilt."

He unfolded the blanket and covered his daughter's head. "We need to get the hell out of here. Fast."

"You lead, I'll follow."

He relocked the safe room and sprinted down the stairs, taking them two at a time. Anna held his neck so tightly, it made it hard to breathe. At the bottom step, he paused at the sight of his best friend's dead eyes. Rina had been part of his life for ten years. No one knew him like she did.

When he stepped out of her life so she could have the type of relationship he couldn't give her, they found a new depth to their friendship. In a split second, it was all gone. Raw, murderous fury filled him with dark thoughts of revenge intermingled with sorrow and regret.

"Adam?"

There wasn't time for hatred or mourning. He headed down the hallway through the kitchen. The door to the basement stood slightly open.

Raw panic hit his stomach. He twisted and glared around the room. When Calista began to speak, he held up his hand, and shook his head.

The scene in front of him wasn't Ludis's style. He never left anything for chance. But this time, he was all over Rina's home. How would Ludis make sure there was nothing to find?

Then it hit him. The answer was so clear. "Son of a bitch."

He grabbed hold of Calista's forearm, rushed into the kitchen, and stopped near the back door. He then peeled Anna's arms from around his neck and leaned close to Calista's ear. "I need to check something. Take Anna, but don't let her remove the quilt."

He eased the basement door open and raced down the stairs. It took only a moment to find Ludis's little package. Enough C-4 to blow the house to hell and back. How long before Ludis set off the C-4 was anyone's guess.

It took him less than five seconds to get back to Calista.

"Adam, what's wrong? Tell me."

25

They were on borrowed time. "I need you to take her to the car. Backtrack through the neighbor's yard. Stay in the shadows."

Calista's eyes widened. "She doesn't know me."

It took everything in him to keep from shoving her out the door. Adam didn't have time to be nice. He had one job, protect Anna and Calista. He removed a corner of the blanket from Anna's face. "Sweetie, this is Calista. She'll take care of you." He leaned down and kissed her cheek.

"Don't leave me."

Adam rubbed his temple when a sharp pain pierced through the back of his head and he met the wide, frightened eyes of his little girl. "I need to take care of your mommy and the house." With a nod to Calista, he recovered Anna with the blanket, and opened the back door.

He took a moment to watch Calista until she was out of sight before he entered the living room and knelt next to Rina. A raw, piercing grief cut deep into his heart.

"We ... You were safe here." His voice broke. He swallowed before removing the small pearl ring on her left finger and the medallion from around her neck. He shoved them in his coat pocket. With one last caress against her cheek, he rose and wiped down the surfaces he touched. Less than a minute later, he opened the fuse box panel door in the kitchen, flipped the switch he had added months before, and shut the door. If Ludis blew the house, the safe room would go up with it. By the time forensic identified all the human remains and discovered Anna wasn't among the dead, Ludis and Emil Vasnev would no longer be a threat to anyone.

Calista had just closed the passenger door with Anna in her lap when he joined them. He soundlessly opened the back door of the sedan.

"Calista, please get in the back." He lifted Anna out of her arms. When she was settled, he set Anna back on her lap, buckling them both in the same safety belt. "Keep your heads below the window."

He shut the door and ran around the back of the sedan to the driver's door. He got in, started the car, and pulled away from the curb without headlights. After coming to a silent stop at the end of the block, his eyes met Calista's. "I'll explain everything. I promise I'll explain."

Just as he turned the corner, a blast ricocheted throughout the quiet neighborhood, shaking the ground. The small home erupted into flames and lit up the night sky in an orange glow. Debris scattered into the street as windows rattled and cracked, setting off several home security alarms throughout the block.

A heart-wrenching moan escaped Anna's lips. Calista raised her head and peered out the back window. "Good God, Adam. What the hell just happened?"

"Head down, Calista." He winced at the harshness in his tone, but he didn't bother to retract it. Their gazes met in the rearview mirror. Not even the fear in her eyes could convince him to put their lives in any more danger when every second counted. How did it get so fucked up?

He turned another corner and wound his way out of the neighborhood. When several police cruisers barreled toward him, he eased over to the side of the road. Once the emergency vehicles passed, he switched on his headlights, pulled out onto Connecticut Avenue, and took the exit onto the Beltway.

"Adam?" Her voice was breathless. "Did you ..."

"No. Ludis."

Color drained from her face as she held Anna close to her. "He blew up the house knowing ...?"

"He wants us both gone."

"Why?"

"We're in the way of what he considers his."

"But she's just a little girl."

"And my daughter. Anna is my daughter."

Chapter Three

Anna is my daughter.

Those three words roiled inside Calista's head. Crouched down in the backseat of Adam's sedan, she could only see the interstate lights zoom past the rear window. She had no idea why she had to hide. If the man who ran from the house doubled back, he would have seen her and Anna get into the vehicle.

In the last thirty minutes, one solid fact hit her square in the face. She had no idea who Adam Blake was—except that he loved his little girl and he could kill a man with his bare hands.

The images of blood and death would be with her for a long time. But it didn't matter that her heart beat like a native drum against the wall of her chest. She had to stay calm. The young girl in her arms needed her.

Anna lay across her chest, motionless except for the involuntary quivering. The back of her little head dampened Calista's thin T-shirt. Shifting her numb left arm, she repositioned Anna into a more comfortable position and draped the lightweight quilt around her shoulders. She couldn't help running her hand over the child's hair, giving her comfort—though nothing she did would ever replace what Anna just lost.

"Calista."

Adam's voice was rough without any sign of humor. She met his gaze in the rearview mirror.

"Still think of me as Batman?"

She stared back at him. He was waiting for a response, but she didn't have one to give. So much had changed since she teased him about having a bat cave. But had anything about the man really changed?

Like her grandfather, Adam moved like a well-trained soldier. He fought like a warrior, killed like a warrior. But the man she stared at in the mirror was no killer. He possessed too great a love for this child.

"Don't do that, Adam. Don't try to make me fear you."

He wanted her to walk away. Well, that wasn't happening. Her instincts never failed her. Adam Blake was one of the good guys regardless of what took place in that home. He would no doubt need a witness on his side of the courtroom if it came to that. Or even just a sympathetic shoulder when he was ready to pick up the pieces. She knew all about that.

She broke eye contact and glanced at the child in her arms. "My life is an open book. You knew who I was the minute we met. In the last half hour, I met another side of Adam Blake and maybe that evens the tables a little." Their gazes reconnected. "But if you don't want me with you and Anna, take me back to the diner. Pete should still be there."

Her words sounded bold, even daring. If he did what she suggested, it would be the last time she ever saw him. A growing ache of loneliness settled in the pit of her stomach.

Adam slowed the speed of the car and exited off the Beltway onto US 1 about five blocks from the diner. Calista's heart skipped a beat. She'd played her only card, a miserable bluff, and it was about to kick her right in the ass.

He drove about a block and pulled into the parking lot of a large chain hotel. He backed into a parking spot at the back of the lot. Calista stared at the dense trees outside the rear window and raised her head to get a better look.

"Why are we stopping here?" Her voice cracked. She cleared her throat as she sat up straighter.

His glare bore into her with such intensity that she almost looked away. Anna seemed to tremble a little harder in her arms. Calista tucked the quilt around her and drew her close to her chest. When he finally spoke, the roughness in his voice made her shiver.

"I'm dropping you off. You can't go home just yet. You'll stay here until I'm sure you're safe."

"No. I'm not staying here."

Adam raised his hand, rotating it so she saw all sides. The blood had dried in an abstract pattern that shifted as his hand twisted.

"My life. Open your eyes, Calista. Nothing about me is safe. It hasn't been for a long time. I couldn't even see my daughter like a normal dad but had to sneak visits behind walls of steel. I was trying to fix that, but after tonight ... "

"Adam." Calista placed her hand on his shoulder. She didn't know what to do, what to say. He was clenching his jaw so hard, a small pulse appeared above his jawbone. She removed her hand and cradled his daughter.

He had returned to his death grip on the steering wheel and peered out into the night. "I should have never allowed it to get this complicated." He raised his bloodied arm. "This isn't your life, Calista. You can leave. So far, no one knows anything about you. If you stay ... " His voice broke.

Calista could hear Adam rub his palm back and forth over his pant leg. It was as if he were trying to wipe away the bloodstain.

A long, low sigh escaped his lips as he rubbed his hand across his forehead. "I won't ask you to leave, but make damn sure you don't have any illusions about me. If you come with us, understand what you're walking into."

The words *hide* and *run* pounded in her head. If she turned her back on Adam and the violence in his world, in a year's time, tonight would play back as a bad dream, a figment of her imagination. Calista glanced down at Anna and her heart warmed.

Her gaze caught the slight glimmer of her wrist bracelet. Hanna use to wear one very similar. Just eyeing the bracelet brought her friend closer. Hanna would never walk away from a child in need. Calista had no idea where the fierce resolve came from, but there was no way she could leave either Anna or Adam until she knew they both were safe.

"I'm with you."

He said nothing for a long time. Anna twisted in her lap and stared at the back of her dad's head.

"No, Anna. I won't stop. She needs to be scared."

Was Adam going into shock or were his senses shutting down? Anna hadn't spoken a word.

"Who needs to be scared?" Calista whispered.

"You do, Calista.. You could have been killed. I told you to drive away."

A moment went by in silence. Then Adam rolled his eyes and a frustrating groan escaped from the back of his throat. He twisted in his seat and addressed his daughter. "Animals get mad, sweetheart. People get angry, pissed. And for the record, I don't care if she's pissed."

The pulse at Calista's neck began to drum. She just shifted a giant step beyond concerned.

"Adam, what's going on?"

"Anna just asked me not to piss you off." His head tilted and his eyes narrowed. "Is there something wrong, Calista?"

"Uh … yeah … maybe. Anna hasn't spoken a word since I met her."

"Yes she has. She doesn't want you to leave. She likes you."

Calista hugged Anna closely. "I like her too, but she hasn't uttered a sound since we met."

"That's impossible." Adam opened the door, got out, and yanked opened the passenger door. He knelt down so he was eye to eye with his daughter. "Anna, say something. Talk to me."

Anna stiffened in Calista's arms but didn't make a sound. Adam raked his hands through his hair and continued to stare at his daughter.

For the next couple of minutes, two identical pair of eyes—father and daughter—glared at each other, but neither spoke. Calista recognized the signs that Adam's headache was back. A strange thought popped into her head.

"Is your head throbbing again?"

"Yes." He rubbed his temples. His gaze never left his daughter's.

"How are you doing this, sweetie?"

Anna shrugged and her eyes grew wide.

"Why won't you speak to me like you always do?"

Anna's body tensed and she began to tremble as she shook her head back and forth. She opened her mouth, but not a sound came out. The more agitated she became, the more color seemed to drain from Adam's cheeks until his complexion was almost waxy. He closed his eyes, held his head in his hands, and sucked in a breath.

Calista moved her hand up Adam's arm and around his neck, massaging the tense neck muscles. "Is she speaking to you right now?"

"Yes ... in my head. I don't know how she's doing this." Pain distorted his features.

Calista's heart dropped to her stomach. Watching the soundless communication pass between Adam and Anna was the most bizarre thing she had ever witnessed.

"Has this telepathic thing between you ever happened before tonight?"

"No."

Calista touched Anna's chin with the tip of her finger and lifted it so their eyes met. "Anna. I want you to try something for me. When you speak to your dad, sing the words in your head."

"Why should she sing?" Adam's fingers dug into the soft skin of his temples, rotating the tips in tight circles.

"The suggestion is totally out of my expertise—anyone's expertise. I think if she changes the frequency of her pitch, the vibration, maybe the headaches will lessen." She glanced down at Anna. "Try it. Instead of talking to your father, sing the words in your head."

The inside of the vehicle grew quiet. Moments later, Adam reached for his daughter's hand. "I understand that, Anna, but ..."

A hallow moan came from deep within his throat, and again, the color drained from his face. He yanked his hand away and cupped his head.

Calista placed her hand on Adam's arm. "What's happening?"

"Anna doesn't want me to leave you here. She thinks it's unsafe." A tear mixed with water and blood escaped the corner of Adam's eyes.

"Sweetie, please sing to your dad." Calista had no idea how to explain to a four-year-old that the words she was telepathically transferring to her father were hurting him. Calista hugged Anna. "I promise you, Anna, I won't leave you until you're ready for me to go."

"Damn it, Calista. Don't promise her that!"

Anna struggled until Calista released her. She flew into her father's arms, almost knocking him to the ground of the parking lot. She placed her hands on either side of his face. The child was doing something right because the tension eased from Adam's eyes and his color returned.

He remained silent, studying his daughter for several moments. When he spoke, his voice was rough. "Fine. I won't leave her here."

Adam grimaced and placed Anna in the backseat. A slight smile formed at the corners of Anna's mouth before she gave her dad a hard hug. After she released him, she moved close to Calista.

He stood and moved behind the sedan. She heard him open the trunk and then the sound of several zippers being ripped open followed by rustling. He must be rummaging through the large duffle she'd noticed when Adam placed her cello in the trunk.

Before she could determine what was happening, Adam slid into the backseat. Without touching Calista, he ran a small device the size of a cell phone up and down Calista's body. Lifting her feet off the floorboard, he ran the device over the soles of her shoes. He repeated the search on his daughter.

"What are you doing?" she asked. She couldn't take her eyes off the device in Adam's hand.

"Looking for tracking devices."

"On me?"

His stare met hers and shrugged. He stopped when a quiet gasp escaped his daughter's lips. "It's okay, Anna. You're safe. I promise you I'll keep you safe."

"Can a tracking device fit anywhere?" Calista lifted Anna into her lap. For some reason, the shivers returned. The little girl was scared and Calista didn't know what to do to ease her fears.

"Yes. Why?"

"What about the items from the room and the backpack?"

"Ludis wasn't in that room."

He stepped outside and lifted the cello case and backpack from the trunk. He ran his device over all of their contents. Leaving the trunk open, he moved back around to the passenger door.

"Calista, please step out of the car." He reached in and placed his hand on his daughter's head. "She's not going anywhere. Promise."

Anna released her grip around Calista's neck and shifted off her lap. Calista took in a deep breath and left the car. The cool breeze caught a few strands of her hair and blew them across her face. She removed a band from around her wrist, pulled the mass of curls into a messy ponytail, and tied it back.

The scent of pine and dirt assaulted her senses, while the concert of crickets and other night creatures remained strangely hushed. Again Calista wondered what they knew that she didn't.

He reached for her hand and placed a handgun in her palm. "Do you really know how to handle a weapon?" His voice was low.

She nodded and swallowed. How she hated the weight of a gun in her hands. But with practiced ease, she removed the magazine and the slide assembly, then replaced the parts without breaking eye contact with Adam. "I've been going to the firing range since I was eleven. Pete made sure I knew how to hold and clean a gun."

He stepped away from the door and handed her the keys. "If you are coming with us, we take only what's on us." He nodded toward the hotel. "My company rents a couple of rooms here. I can store our belongings, but I need you to stay with Anna."

"But wouldn't your sensor pick up any tracking devices?"

"Yes, but all our belongings need to be left here. The lighter we travel, the easier it will be to disappear."

Calista swallowed a lump of fear and got behind the wheel. "Of course. We'll be fine."

"Is there anything in your belongings you have to have?" His gaze fell on her cello, canvas bag of books, and laptop.

"My cello. It's my grandmother's."

Adam placed it back into the trunk. "If I'm not back in five minutes, get the hell out of here. There is an untraceable bank card in the glove compartment as well as cash."

He took out a pen from his coat pocket. Lifting Calista's hand, he scribbled something on the inside of her wrist. It tickled, but her nerves were too raw to laugh.

"Only five minutes, Calista. If I'm not back, leave. I'll find you." He reached into the car and keyed in an address into the GPS. "I'll meet up with you here. The priest is a good friend of mine. If he isn't there," he said, raising her wrist, "trust only this man."

"I can trust Pete."

"But Pete can't protect you." He tapped her wrist. "This man can and will." In a deep, hoarse whisper, he said, "Please take care of my daughter."

Adam didn't wait around for her response, but grabbed their belongings and jogged across the parking lot. Calista followed his progress until he disappeared into the entrance of the hotel. She glanced at the clock on the dashboard. Could she really leave him here?

Calista met Anna's wide-eyed stare in the mirror. "It's going to be okay, Anna. Your dad will be right back."

Anna moved her head back and forth. She fumbled with the seatbelt clip until she had it undone, and climbed over the console into Calista's lap, burying her head in her chest.

"It's going to be okay," she said again, cradling the child in her arms. Taking in a calming breath, she began to hum her favorite childhood lullaby, never taking her eyes off the clock.

Four minutes and thirty-seven seconds later, a black CR-V with no headlights pulled right behind them. Calista's heart dropped to her stomach. Where in hell did it come from?

She didn't hear a thing. It had to be Adam because Anna didn't react. But God, what if it wasn't? When someone stepped out of the vehicle, all Calista could make out was a general height and build.

"Anna, I need you to crawl onto the floorboard of the backseat. Now."

She helped ease Anna over the console. As soon as she was lying prone on the floor, Calista reached for the Glock with her left hand and placed her right hand on the keys in the ignition.

Adam stuck his head into the back window.

"Shit, Adam. You almost made me pee my pants." Calista charged out of the car, one hand planted on her hip while the other gripped the weapon.

He placed his hand lightly on the gun, lowering the barrel to the ground. "Let go, Calista." He gently pried it from her hand. "I'm sorry I startled you."

He stuck the gun into his holster strapped at his side. A slight grin touched the corners of his lips. She wanted to punch him, hard. He didn't look sorry at all.

When he opened the back door, his daughter flew into his arms. He grabbed her stuffed elephant, quilt, and backpack, then faced Calista.

"I want you to rethink going with us. If this hotel doesn't work for you, I have several safe houses I can hide you in until I figure out if your identity has been compromised. You don't have to give up anything. In a couple of days, you can return to your life and this will just be a bad dream."

Her temper rose, but she banked it down. "Do you want me to just walk away from you and Anna?" A cold chill settled deep inside her. A soft hand touched Calista's cheek. With her other hand, Anna grasped hold of Calista's hand so tightly, it almost hurt. Calista brushed the hair off Anna's face. "Talk to me. Tell me what I can do."

Anna flung herself into Calista's arms, wrapping her arms and legs tightly around her.

"It's okay. I'm not going anywhere." Her gaze held Adam's. "And don't tell me you don't want me mixed up in your problems. I'm right smack in the middle of it." She reached into her back pocket of her jeans and pulled out her cell phone. "I forgot I had this on me." She handed it to Adam. "Just toss it."

His face grew tense. In fact, his whole body was one hard, taut muscle, but his eyes held a deep retching sadness. He reached over and tried to take Anna, but she wouldn't let go. He let out a sigh and stepped back.

"Baby girl, let go of Calista."

But if anything, her grip grew tighter.

"If someone tracked you here, we can't stand around arguing." Calista raised her wrist. "You said this guy could be trusted. If that's so, will it matter if I stay with you for another few hours?"

She swallowed hard, pushing down the fear that seemed to make its home in her gut. Giving up her cell phone meant breaking contact with her world. What if Pete needed her and tried to text her?

"I know it doesn't make any sense, Adam." She paused and swallowed hard. "Anna wants me with you and you can keep us all safe."

"I don't know that, Calista. Damn it, *you* can't know that."

She didn't miss the anguish in his voice. "I'm willing to chance it for Anna."

Maybe Anna's clinging was just a desperate attempt to hold onto another female, a substitute for what she knew she just lost. Calista understood that feeling. She lived it after her parents died in a drunk driver accident when she was only eleven. The pain, the loss never went away.

Caring for the frightened little girl in her arms wasn't a choice but a necessity. She strolled over to the CR-V, cradling Anna close to her chest. "This is the right thing to do right now."

Adam handed her back her cell phone. Calista began to shake her head when his finger touched her lips.

"You need it to stay in touch with Pete."

He removed the plastic cover from the back of her phone. After removing the memory card and battery, he opened the inside panel. He took a small case from his pocket and selected what looked like a tiny pair of tweezers. He plucked off one of the tiny chips and smashed it into the asphalt with his boot heel.

After replacing the battery and memory card, he handed it back to her. "That was the manufacturer's tracking device. It's almost impossible to trace now."

Calista gave him a hard look then began to chuckle. "That's ... "

"Creepy? I know," he said, with a grimace. "Your number will come up on Pete's phone as unknown caller. You will need to check in with him and let him know what's going on."

Calista swallowed a lump just thinking about that conversation. She replaced the phone in her pocket. "Is this yours or are we borrowing it?" she said, nodding at the black CR-V.

He pressed his lips together. "This is a company vehicle. I've spent too many years fighting people who had no respect for the law. I don't break them unless I have to." After opening the back door, he reached for Anna. "Let go, Anna, just long enough for Calista to get settled." Anna released her hold and went into her father's arms.

Calista scooted over to the seat behind the driver. Adam leaned in and set his daughter behind the passenger's seat. She leaned her head down on Calista's lap, using the quilt as a pillow. Adam buckled the seat belt around her and draped his jacket over her shoulders.

Calista fussed with the jacket covering Anna as she ran her hand down the back of the preschooler's hair. Adam placed his hand over hers and held it. She kept her eyes down. It was late and she was tired of arguing with him.

His palm cupped her chin and turned her face to meet his. Instead of an expression of total frustration, his features softened and a tender smile touched the corner of his lips.

"Thank you, Calista … for caring." He lifted his head and his eyes scanned the darkness. "It's been a long time since anyone has worried about me."

His lips brushed across hers with such tenderness, she almost forgot she held his child in her lap. Calista covered her hand over his and deepened the kiss for an instant before he broke away. He stepped back, shutting the door of the CR-V soundlessly. Watching him move around the back of the vehicle, she ran her tongue over her bottom lip. The simple kiss released a hunger in her she didn't know existed. For the first time that evening, she was truly scared.

Chapter Four

As Adam maneuvered through the light traffic on the parkway heading into Washington D.C., his attention drifted between the rained soaked asphalt and the backseat. Calista's lids grew heavy, but she fought sleep. She kept her guard up to protect his daughter. Now his need to keep Calista close competed with his need to keep her safe. She couldn't become another victim of the nightmare that was his life.

His thumb pressed the send icon on his cell phone and the text disappeared off the screen. He waited a moment, but when nothing came back, he resent the text. *Fuck, Colin. Answer me!*

Colin White never ignored Adam's texts. His partner had worked the protection detail with Adam earlier that evening and offered to replace their gear in the secure storage unit then return to the office to take care of the after action report. That was usually Adam's responsibility, but Colin pushed him out the door. He touched the small bandage on his forehead. The earlier evening events seemed like a lifetime ago.

Adam coded in a number on his cell phone and the surveillance footage at the unit popped on the screen. Everything looked fine. He then tried the code for his offices. Nothing. After several tries, he shut the phone off and tossed it into the seat next to him.

"I can hear you grinding your teeth all the way back here."

He smiled, but it did nothing to ease the strain from Calista's eyes. "I need to check in at the office. Why don't you try closing your eyes for a few minutes?"

"What's wrong?"

"Nothing, or at least nothing new."

"Adam?"

He let out a shaky, frustrated groan. "My partner isn't responding to my texts. I need to check on him."

"Do you think Ludis ..."

"I don't know, Calista. It'll take at least twenty minutes to drive into DuPont Circle. Please try to sleep."

"I want to keep you company." Her words trailed away as her eyelids closed, popped back open, and then closed again. Not wanting to be alone with his thoughts, Adam almost woke her up, a selfish act for his own sanity.

He grieved for Rina, though he could never define what she meant to him. They were a team, Rina, Colin, and him. As operatives, they understood and accepted each other. They were closer than most siblings, but also strangers to each other. Off the job, they had their separate lives until the day Adam and Rina became a couple, and then had to disappear.

Of course, then the CIA wanted answers. Colin was left to deal with the fallout, answering questions that didn't have answers while relaying insider information on the investigation to his colleagues in hiding. He retired three years later and opened the security firm with Adam as his very silent partner.

Adam worked selective assignments, the man the staff referred to in the corridors as Colin's ghost. They weren't far off on that assessment. He did stalk the offices late at night when no one was around. When Colin refused to discuss him, the employees came up with their own stories about Adam's role in the company.

Adam glanced down at his quiet cell phone in the passenger seat and cringed. Something was definitely wrong. A heavy, relentless sense of dread settled over him. Pressing on the accelerator, he maneuvered around several cars and hitched his speed to a good twenty miles over the speed limit.

While the road held no interest, the adrenaline pumping through his veins kept Adam's mind on high alert when all he wanted to do was shut down. As a damn good strategist, he never needed his skills more than now. But for his mind to work, he had to let go the images of Rina lying in her own blood, staring into nothingness.

Hatred churned in the pit of his stomach, curling acid into his throat. He clamped down on his jaw and the tension shot straight to his head. But that was okay with him. He needed the pain.

God ... Rina. How was he going to survive without her?

It took ten years, but Rina was the only woman who knew him completely—secrets, nightmares, everything. And that information got her gutted like a fucking fish. He removed his cramped right hand from the steering wheel and stretched out his fingers. He tried to rub the red stain off the palm of his hand, but Rina's blood appeared to have permanently marked his skin.

As he made his way into the center of downtown D.C., he eased off the foot pedal and traveled into DuPont Circle. Adam pulled off the circle onto a side street. The odd triangular shape building that housed the firm was dark, quiet. Several cars were parked in the small-gated parking lot, where he spotted Colin's black Miata immediately. The only reason his friend wouldn't answer Adam's call was that he couldn't.

There was no way he could leave Anna and Calista in the car while he checked out the offices on the sixth floor. Without stopping, he made his way out of the city, pulling into one of the lighted parking spots at the New Carrollton metro station fifteen minutes later. He took great care opening the door without a sound so as not to wake Calista and Anna. He unlocked the trunk and pulled out Calista's laptop. A few minutes on the computer would confirm what his heart already mourned.

It took seconds to break through Calista's security code. Breaching Colin's security measures to access the main controls took a little longer. Once he had control of the building's camera footage, he worked his way through the firm, room by room until he reached the inner office. Adam had set those cameras himself. With one final click, his heart dropped into the pit of his stomach.

Colin sat at his desk, his face beaten beyond recognition. His body was strapped into the chair with coils. Ludis had used a battery to torture his friend before he placed a bullet between his eyes.

Adam slammed the laptop and practically threw it into the trunk. He eased back into the car for his cell phone and called 911. He couldn't save his friend, but he sure as hell wasn't going to leave him alone until the staff showed up.

His friends were dead. Why was Ludis so desperate to find him that he would go to these lengths?

"Are you okay, Daddy?"

Anna's soft voice broke through his anger. He glanced at the rearview mirror and met her gaze. "I'm fine, sweetheart. Go back to sleep."

Her lower lip quivered as her eyes filled with tears. *"I want Mommy."*

Adam swallowed a lump and clenched his jaw, his teeth grinding into the enamel. "I know, sweetie. She didn't want to leave you."

He swallowed again, hard. This time his teeth bit the tender skin inside his mouth, drawing the metallic taste of blood. "She loves you, baby girl. Very much."

Anna nodded and let out a shaky sigh. By some miracle, his words gave her some comfort because she laid her head on Calista's lap and closed her eyes. Moments later, her breathing slowed and she drifted back to sleep.

Adam had never felt so damn helpless in his life. He had no idea how to help his daughter. She had to be in shock and in need of medical attention, the kind he was ill-equipped to give her.

The crazy telepathy ... where in the hell did that come from? How was she able to let him know Rina needed him? If it wasn't for the lingering pain that pulsed from his frontal lobe to the back of his head, he could easily believe he had finally plunged into the deep end of insanity.

But Anna was communicating with him through her thoughts. He was going to have to get his little girl to open up to him. How much did she witness? Did Ludis see her? Could she identify Ludis? Did she witness that bastard hurting her mother? He needed to know what she knew.

Adam worked his way around the Beltway to the Washington/Baltimore parkway. Once in Baltimore, he exited onto Pratt Street. He rolled his shoulders as his mind settled on one conclusion: he'd fucked up somewhere and led Ludis right to Rina's and Anna's doorstep. Anna was motherless because of him. He rubbed his abdomen with a slow circular motion and welcomed the churning acid. It was his penance, and he didn't care if it ate him alive from the inside out.

Calista jolted awake. "Where are we?"

"Baltimore. We're about five minutes from a bed."

He slowed as he drove through downtown past Camden Yards, Inner Harbor, and into Fells Point where he turned into a large empty church parking lot. He cut the headlights, maneuvered around the back of the church, and backed into the darkest spot, facing the two-story rectory.

"Why are we stopping at a Catholic church?" she asked, unable to hide the fatigue in her voice from him.

Adam paused. How much of his plan should he share with Calista? "I have a friend here who can help us, but I need to check it out first. Lay Anna on the seat and come up front."

Calista did what he asked and crawled over the console into the passenger seat. He reached for her hand and held it between his two large hands. "Same rules apply as at the hotel. If I'm not back in five minutes, get the hell out of here."

He nodded toward an alley off the back of the lot. He caressed the number he penned on her wrist with his thumb. "Take the alley to Pratt. Keep your lights off. Find a place to lay low and contact the man on your wrist."

He pulled the Glock from his holster and set it on the driver's seat. He watched as Calista swallowed. Fear etched in her eyes and he wanted to kick himself. His first mistake—he should have hurled Calista's butt out of his car on the damn entrance ramp, called her a cab, and drove away. And what was he thinking giving into Anna's pleas? It was a little late to earn Father of the Year votes.

"Calista, this is a safe place. I'm just being cautious."

Adam exited the vehicle, shutting the door without so much as a click. He kept to the shadows, working around the shrubs that surrounded the porch. Nothing felt out of the ordinary. He pulled out a pick and had the door unlocked in seconds. With one quick glance at the CR-V and the lot, he slipped into the dark foyer.

The familiar waxy scent of linseed and lavender oils filled his nostrils. It took a moment for his eyes to adjust to the darkness. A hardwood floor beam creaked and the silhouette of a man appeared in the doorway of the living room. He clenched the butt of his weapon but kept it pointing down at his side.

"Relax, Adam. It's me." The man was dressed in black pants and a black clerical shirt with a white plastic strip at the collar. "I have a doorbell, you know."

The tension drained from his body. "Sorry, Robert. It hasn't been a good night. Are things good here?"

The priest stiffened and nodded. "What's going on?"

Adam raised his hand and reached for the door. "I'm not alone. Give me a sec."

He left the rectory as quietly as he entered. This time he called out to Calista as he approached the car. "It's me," he said, and opened the back door of the vehicle. He reached in and carefully lifted Anna into his arms. She wrapped her hands around his neck and set her head on his shoulder but remained asleep. Calista scrambled for the quilt and stuffed elephant, got out on her side, and moved around to the back of the CR-V. Adam opened the trunk and reached for Calista's cello, but she grabbed the handle first.

"I got it, Calista."

"Yes, but I've been tugging this around since fourth grade. You have your hands full."

"Is there some personal reason you can't follow the simplest order? If there is, I really need to know that now."

Her eyes narrowed and she yanked the cello from the trunk. "My cello, my responsibility. I'm not a soldier and this isn't the military. And since when do I take orders from you?"

"The instant you got out of that damn car." Adam took her hand and practically dragged her into the home. As soon as he closed the front door, Robert lifted a strand of hair off the child's face and gasped.

"Good God. Is this Anna?"

"Yes. This is my daughter." He drew Calista close to him. "And this is Calista Martin."

The priest took a moment to study Calista before he raked both hands through his hair. He reached for her hand. "It's a pleasure to meet you. I'm Father Robert Anthony, but everyone calls me Anthony." He glanced at Adam and said, "Except this guy."

He turned toward Adam. "It really hasn't been a good night, has it?"

Adam shook his head.

"What can I do?"

Adam handed him the keys to the CR-V. "Move the vehicle while I put Anna down."

The priest took the keys. "Make yourself at home." He nodded toward the second floor. "You know where the guest room is." He turned and left the house.

Adam placed his free arm around Calista's shoulder. A shiver raced through her body and into Adam's heart. In his saner moments, when he wasn't trying to stay alive, he could appreciate the misguided instincts that landed her in the middle of his hell. Years ago, that could have been him.

"I had my reasons for getting out of the car, Adam. I'm not a complete idiot."

He gently pulled her into an embrace, totally expecting her to punch him in the gut. Shockingly, she laid her head against his chest, circled his waist with one hand, and hugged Anna with the other.

"God, Calista. I'm sorry … it wasn't supposed to be like this. Your night wasn't supposed to turn into … *this*."

They stood quietly for several moments until he broke the silence. He placed his hand on her cheek. "You're safe for the moment. We're all safe here."

"Your friend—a priest? I wasn't expecting that."

Adam chuckled. "He's my old commanding officer. The closest thing to *Batman* you're ever gonna meet."

"I don't understand."

"Don't let the collar fool you. He's a one-man army when he has to be." He sighed and rubbed his tired eyes with his fingertips. "But Robert left that life behind when he entered the seminary and doesn't like it when he has to revisit it. We'll only stay here tonight."

He took a step toward the staircase and repositioned Anna in his arms. "As soon as I get Anna settled, we can talk. I'm sure you have some questions."

Calista followed Adam to the second floor. He opened the door at the end of the hallway and laid Anna in one of the two twin beds, covering her with the quilt. He removed a loose strand of hair from her cheek, slipping it behind her small ear, and tucked the stuffed elephant in her arms.

"Rina made the blanket with some of Anna's old baby clothes." He stood and rubbed the back of his neck. "I have a couple of picture albums and few odds and ends, but not much to show for her mother's life."

Calista ran her hand over the stitching on the bottom corner of the quilt. "It's beautiful. Anna will cherish it." She glanced up at Adam. "She doesn't need boxes of her mom's stuff to remember her. What you've collected will be enough as long as you ..."

Calista lowered her head and shifted.

Damn, had he been such an intimidating jerk that now she didn't feel she could be open with him? Keeping her safe would be almost impossible if they couldn't communicate.

He placed a hand on her arm. "As long as I what?"

She cleared her throat and swiped at a lone tear. "Share Rina with Anna. She needs to be able to talk about her mother with you. That is how she will heal—spending time with you, talking about the woman you both loved."

Adam moved toward the window. From the corner of his eye, he watched his daughter's chest rise and fall in a blissful sleep. Every ounce of love he had for her gripped his heart in a vise lock of regret. "That's not possible. She's safer away from me."

"Well, damn it, Adam, make it possible. You're all she has left. If not you, then who?" Calista tucked the covers around Anna's shoulders. "She is all that matters now. She needs *you.*"

Adam leaned his head against the cool glass of the window, eyeing the quiet neighborhood. How in the hell was he going to justify his plan for Anna to Calista?

He knew a little of Calista's story through Pete. She lost her parents at a young age. She understood exactly what his little girl was feeling. Calista's choice to stay with him tonight was pure, heartfelt emotion. Adam spent years alone and kept a tight clamp on his emotions. He functioned on reason except when it came to Anna—and apparently Calista.

But that had to change. He had to keep his heart out of the equation to keep Anna safe. Calista was the type of woman who would never forgive him for walking away from his own daughter. But to keep Anna alive, that was exactly what he planned to do.

He cleared his throat. "I have never lived with Anna. While I saw her as much as I thought safe, we've never been out of Rina's home together. I don't know how to help her ... raise her."

"Learn how, Adam."

She made it sound so easy. *If you want something badly enough, you can make it happen.* Maybe in Calista's normal world, life worked like that. It sure the hell didn't happen in the one he lived.

"I know how to hunt down the men who killed Rina. I can extract information from them and discover where Ludis is hiding. I can kill Ludis with these," he said, lifting his hands.

"Adam ..."

"No, Calista. That's exactly what has to happen. This nightmare that's my life has gone on too long. It's time to end it."

She let out a shaky breath. "Then end it. Do what you have to do and come back to Anna." Her eyes narrowed. "Who is Ludis? Rina mentioned another name, Vasnev."

She had no business knowing about his other life. But now that she was in the middle of it, she had to understand what he was up against—what *she* was up against if she decided to stay with him.

"Ludis is my uncle, my mother's brother." Calista stiffened, though he doubted she did it consciously. "The other man, Emil Vasnev, is my grandfather. My mother hid me from her family to protect me from their world. But like me, she couldn't stay away from her only child."

He cracked open the window. The musky scent from the harbor filled his lungs. He took in another breath of the evening breeze and tried to slam the door to his memory of the last time he saw his mother alive.

Annija Vasnev had brought him into the world, and then sacrificed everything so his life would be different than hers.

But their lives weren't different. Tonight, their lives mirrored each other.

"My Aunt Annija was my favorite person in the world. I had no idea she was my mother." He let the silence soothe him a moment. "My grandfather controls the most brutal crime syndicate in Eastern Europe. His hand reaches into every major government in the world. There isn't anything he hasn't done. Ludis, his only son, is his right hand. If my mother gave birth to me under her father's roof, Emil Vasnev would have owned me. So she ran, found a couple to raise me as their own. But like I did, she led Vasnev and Ludis right to me."

Adam never shared the first time he came up against Ludis with anyone. How he found his adoptive parents tied up, tortured—dead.

His parents were a kind, soft-spoken couple who spent their days unearthing lost cultures. They never had a bad thing to say about anyone. To live their last moments on earth with a man like Ludis Vasnev was unthinkable. The only reason Adam hadn't put a bullet between his uncle's eyes years ago was because Rina stopped him, told him he was a better man than that.

"Ludis must have tracked Annija's numerous visits. The day my parents and Annija died, I had just turned eighteen and was clueless to the secrets surrounding my birth."

A rush of hatred gushed through his veins as his heart thumped between his ears. *Fuck being a better man.* He should have killed the bastard the day he learned who he was.

"Annija was too late to save my parents. She handed me a backpack just like this one." He lifted Anna's pack off the floor then dropped it. "She told me to run and I did. She drove away, drawing Ludis away from me, and ended up at the bottom of a canyon."

"My God, Adam. Why?"

"Simple, Calista. Evil breeds evil. My grandfather wants me. I'm a Vasnev, his to control. He sent his trusted son to find me."

He curled his fingers into his palm. He felt Calista place her hand on each of those fists. That simple gesture eased the revulsion crashing through him. He sucked in a breath through his clenched teeth and let it out slowly before he spoke.

"Emil Vasnev is sick, dying. Ludis has just been biding his time until the day he takes control of his father's empire. My mother was in his way." His gaze landed on his sleeping daughter. "Anna and I are now in Ludis's way. Rina knew all of this. That's why we gave up our lives, faked our deaths, and hid Anna." He raked both hands through his hair. He wanted to rip it out by the roots, anything to escape the pain.

"Ludis won't give up. I know his next move and I have to warn them." His hoarse voice fell to a whisper.

"Who?"

"My father's family." He shoved his fisted hands into his pockets. "He'll go after them next. Like my adoptive parents, they will be caught completely unaware."

"I don't understand."

Adam turned from the window and faced Calista. "My father's family … I know who they are and even spend time with them, helping them out when I can." Adam swallowed the lump in his throat before he could continue. "They don't know who I am."

"Wait, your father knows you, but doesn't know you're his son?"

He could only nod. "My mom never contacted him when she discovered she was pregnant with me for the same reason she gave me up."

He raised Calista's arm, traced his finger over the phone number he wrote on her skin and cleared his throat. "But that last day, she gave me his number just like this, and told me if ever I needed him, he would help." He fixed her with a stare. "Rina and I chose to live in this area so I could be close to my father. I wanted to look out for him and his family in case they ever needed me."

Adam leaned both hands on the windowsill. His fingernails bit into the old wood. "Now I have placed his entire family in the line of fire."

"His family? You mean you have brothers ... sisters ...?"

"Four half-brothers and one half-sister. And I'm about to rip their world wide open."

Chapter Five

Adam stood at the window, his body tense, and a hard tightness around his eyes. The walls of the small, sparsely furnished guest room appeared to close in on him. He was so closed off, Calista didn't dare approach him.

Anna moaned and shifted slightly in her sleep. It was if she could feel her father's anguish. After the bizarre evening Calista just lived through, she didn't doubt the telepathic connection also gave her access into his emotional state—a lot for a four-year-old little girl to deal with.

Calista knelt by the twin bed and placed her hand on Anna's shoulder. An instant later, Anna's breathing slowed and she settled back into a deep, restful sleep.

Adam hadn't moved. He continued to glare out the window with his back to her. If a simple gesture of a hand on a shoulder helped Anna, maybe it would help her dad.

Calista took a calming breath and approached the window. She reached out and placed her hand on his arm. When he didn't yank away from her touch, she eased closer, bringing both hands around his waist. She then rested her head against his back, hugging him close to her. With her ear against his back, she could feel each frantic heartbeat.

He was in pain and Calista didn't have a clue how to help him. He gave up a relationship with Rina, his daughter, his father, his family. What other sacrifices had he made?

"Are you wishing I'd never walked into Pete's diner?" His rich baritone voice was so low, his words came out in a hoarse whisper.

"No, of course not." Calista reached inside Adam's sport coat and removed the photo she'd seen him take from Anna's safe room. "Who took this picture of Rina and Anna at the zoo?"

He didn't respond for a long time. "I did."

"But you didn't go with them or meet them there. Instead you watched over them, alone, out of sight." She stopped, trying to find the right words.

"This photo tells a story about you, Adam, about the kind of man you are. Just like in the photo, you stand on the outside looking in, taking care of everyone. You feel you're responsible for the people you love, responsible for taking down the evil who threatens them." She let out a heavy sigh. "Well, there must be a way to remove Ludis's threat and still be able to live a normal life with your daughter."

"Calista, my life doesn't work that way. There are no Pollyanna solutions that will fix everything."

She couldn't help grinning. Pete called her Pollyanna all the time. "There is if you take a minute and look for one. There has to be someone who can help you, someone you trust to have your back. I'll have your back if you let me."

"Hell no! You're not going anywhere near those bastards, Calista."

He kept his arms to his side, but Calista could feel how badly he wanted to shove past her. She held up her hands, but instead of stepping back like her mind screamed for her to do, she eased her body closer, drawing him into her arms.

"I have no desire to meet that white-haired bastard."

"How in the hell do you know what Ludis looks like?"

Adam's voice turned hard as if all the emotion drained from him and only cold fury filled the void.

"I saw him," Calista said, her eyes on her feet. She quickly counted to ten then faced him. "When he burst out the front door."

This time Adam did grab hold of her and his expression was wild. He wasn't hurting her, but she could sense an incredible control in him.

"Did he see you?"

"No. I hid behind the crape myrtle the instant I heard the door open." She placed her hand on his cheek and massaged the tense vein above his left eye.

"He didn't see me, Adam. He was moving fast, holding his shoulder, and bleeding badly. The whole upper right section of his shirt was beet red." She never wavered from his intense gaze. "He never glanced back. I waited to enter the house after he drove away. I didn't get the license number, but it was a rental tag."

Adam released his hold on her and raked a hand through his hair. He began to pace in the small area near the window, his entire body one tense muscle.

"This is not your fight."

"And it's not just yours either, Adam." Calista swallowed. Maybe she should have kept her opinion to herself, but she acted on emotion, shot from her heart. And that child sleeping in the bed deserved her heart.

"What the hell is that supposed to mean?"

"The way I see it, it became your father's fight the second you were conceived."

Calista placed her hand on his sleeve and he turned to face her. "Yesterday, even a couple hours ago, you could have gone after Ludis and maybe not cared if you came out alive. Everything has changed."

"My father doesn't even know I'm his son."

"Then tell him and then let him help you."

"What makes you think he even has the skill to help me go after Ludis?"

Calista ran her gaze up and down his body. "You can't be *like you* without your father being just as capable as you are. And your brothers … you said you help them when they need it. Well, damn it, it's their turn to step up and help you."

She didn't know how hard to push. Adam was up against a rock and a hard place but she had to get through to him.

"You've had a rough road that I can't possibly understand." She looked over at the sleeping child in the bed and her heart skipped a beat. She knew exactly what Anna was going to go through the moment she woke up: when the reality of last night came crashing down. Adam needed to understand his game had changed. Taking a step closer to him, Calista clamped her hands in front of her and said a quick prayer that her next words wouldn't place a wall between her and Adam they could never tear down.

"Anna needs you more than you need revenge. Your grandfather is dying, and if Ludis is as bad as you say he is, there must be law enforcement agencies around the globe looking for him. Let them have him and you take care of your daughter."

He didn't walk out. Instead he moved in closer, but kept his hands to his side. "I can't do that, Calista." He broke eye contact and glanced at Anna. "There isn't anyone in the world I love more than that little girl. But ... it's my fight. *Not* my father's, *not* my brothers. Mine."

Calista could feel her eyes fill. Her heart hurt with a loss she had never known before. She saw what his uncle was capable of tonight. Adam would never survive on his own against Ludis and his army of killers. And he knew it. He didn't care as long as he rid the threat to Anna.

"Calista, say something. Say you understand." He reached for her clenched hands and held them like they were delicate porcelain.

The first tear fell and she wiped it away on her shoulder. While she couldn't stop the tears, she sure as hell wasn't going to let them sidetrack her from trying to convince Adam where his priorities lay.

"So, tonight, how is this supposed to play out? You're going to kiss your daughter goodnight, maybe give me a peck on the cheek, wait for us to fall asleep, and then just leave?"

The humming of the ceiling fan was the only sound in the room.

"Something like that."

Fury began to burn in the pit of her stomach. "Anna doesn't know me or Father Anthony. How could you do that to her on the day her mom died? You're not *that* man."

An angry, dark hardness edged into Adam's features. "You don't know me, Calista. You don't know what I have done, what I'm capable of doing."

She raised her arms and dropped them to her side. "Boy, do you have that right. The man who hung out at the diner wouldn't be so damn callus to his own daughter."

He took several angry steps away from her. "Good. Hate me. Loathe me. That will make my leaving easier for both of us."

Calista could only stare as tears flowed freely. She swiped them off with the bottom of her T-shirt. "Just make sure you are leaving for the right reasons."

"What the hell is that suppose to mean?"

"Leaving Anna, going off to kill the dragon is a lot easier than staying here and dealing with your emotions about Rina and raising Anna on your own."

Adam's features grew hard and his eyes narrowed. "I'm not a coward."

"I didn't mean to imply … "

"I won't walk away from punishing Ludis myself. I can't involve my father or my brothers either." He cupped her face. "I can't, Calista."

Something in him changed before her eyes. A resolve. His eyes hardened, his jaw clenched. His mind was made up. Any argument from her would fall on deaf ears.

He cleared his throat. "I'll take her to my father. He will adore his granddaughter, and my brothers and sister will spoil her rotten. They all will love Anna, raise her as their own if I can't come back."

Adam reached over and ran a tender hand over the back of his daughter's hair. "I'm not leaving her alone. She will be happy again. They are a great family."

Calista nodded. She almost choked on her next thought—but it was up to her to say it out loud, or she would regret her cowardice forever.

"Take me with you. I can…"

"Calista, you can't go with me. If anything happened to you under my responsibility I would lose the last connection to humanity and become an animal—no better than Ludis Vasnev."

As much as she wanted to give him a good smack, hard enough to make him see reason, she needed to find a logical reason to appeal to him. Before she could seize on her next line of attack, she heard a rustling in the doorway.

Good God. She completely forgot the priest was in the house. How much of their conversation had he heard? "Sorry … we … "

"Don't mind me. I'm used to being ignored by the men in Adam's family." A grin formed at the corner of his lips. "I assume you'll need some sort of disguise for Anna?"

"Yes," Adam said.

The priest nodded. "I'll see what I have in the church. He moved toward the door then turned back. "She's right, you know. I would listen to her if I were you, Adam." He turned and left the room.

Chapter Six

Adam sprinted around the last curve on the bike trail. The old Buick he borrowed from the church lot was parked five blocks away on a busy residential street. Patchy cloud cover and the canopy of leafy trees made his approach almost invisible. The late spring breeze with a hint of woodsy, pine scent permeated the air. It usually had a calming effect on him, but not tonight.

The path he could have run blindfolded. It led to the home of a man Adam had risked his life for and trusted to always have his back.

He bounded over the fence into a yard. The moon bathed the grassy area. Keeping within the shadows of the large oak tree, he made his way onto the patio. A large dog rubbed up against his calf. He reached down and stroked him behind the ears.

"Macy, you're almost as big as a horse. What the hell do they feed you?"

Adam pulled out a dog treat from his coat pocket and fed it to the dog. He gulped it down in one bite then settled back on his blanket. Adam gave him one more rub down before easing toward the back door.

Like the rectory lock, he had this one opened in seconds and stepped into the cool, dark kitchen. He closed the curtain on the door as well as the curtain covering the window above the sink. The kitchen smelled of home cooked meals, laughter, love, family. Everything he wanted for Anna.

The house was asleep. The thought of his daughter still sleeping soundly in the twin bed with Calista back at the rectory pierced a hole in his gut. He'd done exactly what Calista had flung in his face: He waited until they were both were asleep, then kissed Anna on the cheek and left. Robert would help them with their disguises and escort them here. As much as he hated leaving their side, there was no way he could walk into the house with them.

Adam had no idea how much Ludis knew about his family. If his uncle sent his men to watch this home, one woman, a priest who was a dear family friend, and a little boy wouldn't raise any questions.

Reaching for the coffee maker on the counter next to the refrigerator, he set it to brew. He leaned up against the sink and crossed his arms around his middle as his mind ran through the plan. The hardest part would be leaving without Calista and Anna. He had no idea how he was going to accomplish that, but he would because he had no choice.

He opened the cabinet and pulled out a mug. He then reached for the carafe and poured himself a cup full of the strong, aromatic liquid. He raised it to his lips and took a large gulp, allowing the hot brew to flow down his throat into his stomach. In no time, the coffee would mix with the acid and burn like hell, but he needed the caffeine to stay standing.

He was so engrossed in charging his system, the quiet footsteps on the stairs didn't register. When the young woman entered the room, she startled him so, he jerked, spilling half the mug down his white dress shirt.

"Noah, it's O-dark-thirty. What the hell are …?"

The words froze in her throat. She grabbed a knife from the stand on the counter before Adam could reach her and aimed it at his heart.

"Who the hell are you and how did you get in here?"

"Jennie, please don't throw that knife. It'll really hurt."

He eased away from the counter and raised his hands. If Jennie McNeil threw a knife at him, it would land where she aimed.

He didn't need light to feel the fear in the young woman. Her breathing came out in short, shallow breaths. "I'm a friend. Jared's friend. Call him."

"She already did, Adam."

A tall, muscular man stood in the doorway behind his wife brandishing a Beretta. A low growled escaped his throat. "What the hell are you doing creeping around my kitchen scaring Jennie out of her skin?" He released the safety on his weapon and placed it on the counter.

"Jared. Don't. The moron broke into our home. If you don't pound on him, I will."

Adam felt a grin building from the somewhere deep within his bruised heart. How could he forget how fierce Jennie McKenzie McNeil was?

"That message thing between you and Jennie is very impressive. You told me about how you guys feel each other's emotions, but this is the first time I actually witnessed it."

Maybe telepathy was an unknown family trait. He was dying to ask if they had to deal with the mind-blowing headaches, but the question sounded so ridiculous in his own head, he didn't dare.

Jared came up behind Jennie and covered the hand holding the knife. He eased the handle out of her grip and replaced it in the stand. Drawing her back against him, he said, "This is Adam. You don't want to kill him, babe."

"Yeah, I think I do." She glanced back at her husband. "This guy breaks into our home and you're okay with that?

Adam let loose a deep chuckle and relaxed against the counter, taking another large gulp of coffee.

Jennie eyed Adam from head to toe. "I don't know, Jared. He's drinking my coffee at," she glanced at the clock over the stove, "five thirty in the morning."

Adam raised his mug. "I'm really sorry if I woke you. I was hoping to get some shut-eye before you guys woke up."

"Then go home." Jennie grabbed the cup from his hand and set it next to Jared's gun.

Jared brought his mouth next to his wife's ear. "Jennie, this is the man who not only planned my escape during that case in Mexico but carried me out on his back. Give him back his coffee."

Jennie made a sound similar to a growl from a mother lion and reached for the light switch. The kitchen flooded with bright light strong enough to make Adam blink twice. Jennie stepped close to him and studied him from head to toe. Her intense scrutiny made him want to stand straighter and right his collar.

"Who are you?" she asked, her voice low, almost a whisper.

"Adam Blake."

Her gaze went to his eyes and she said nothing for a long time. "No. Who *are* you?"

Adam shrugged, trying not to squirm. He knew there was a family resemblance. All the McNeil men had the same dark, cobalt blue eye color. Until recently, Adam had kept his facial features partially hidden by a thick beard. He also left his dark brown hair long, unkempt, making that particular feature less noticeable.

Jared handed Adam back his coffee and placed an arm around Jennie. "So, Adam, new look? What happened to the Grizzly Adam motif?" he said, nodding at the suit.

Adam scraped his fingernails against the stubble along his jaw. "Got tired of sharing my face with the fleas. Besides, I opened a security firm a few months ago in D.C. The fancy office building my company rents space from took exception to the old me."

Jennie stepped directly in front of him. "Did you really save Jared from Mendoza's hellhole?"

"I got there as quickly as ... "

Her thin frame slammed into his, her arms circling his neck as she hugged the life out of him.

"Thank you, God, thank you." Jennie lifted on her toes and kissed his cheek, twice on each side, ending with a peck on his lips. She dropped her arms and stepped back, her eyes clouded with tears.

"Okay, so whoever you are, you're family for life." Her eyes darted around the room. "What can I get you? Are you hungry? We have everything today." She opened the refrigerator then called back over her shoulder, "You can have almost any breakfast food your heart desires. What can I fix you?"

Jared reached for his wife and moved her out of the doorway of the refrigerator, closing it.

"Jen, I think what Adam needs more than anything are a couple hours of sleep."

"I'm fine," he said. "I don't want to be any trouble."

Jennie's eyes widened as her eyes suddenly landed on the blood on his cuff, following it up his sleeve. "Are you hurt, bleeding?"

Shit.

He completely forgot the condition of his clothing. Shaking his head, Adam said, "No. It's not mine."

"Whose blood is it, Adam?" Jared eyed his jacket and shirtsleeve. The blood blended well into the wool of his black suit.

He let out a heavy sigh. "I ... this is going to be hard to explain," he said, raising the cuff of his right hand. "I didn't start this fight. I just didn't get there in time to do much good."

"Are you hurt?" Jared repeated.

"No."

"Is anyone looking for you?"

"Define anyone."

"The cops, FBI, Homeland Security."

Adam raised both hands. Some explanation was needed, but he didn't have the energy to give Jared what he was asking. "Do we have to do this now?"

"Yes." Jared stiffened, his jaw muscle tense.

"No, we don't, Jared. Adam needs sleep." Jennie placed her hand on her husband's chest.

Jared glanced down at her and a smile appeared at the corner of his lips. "This from a woman who just a couple minutes ago wanted to plunger him with our best kitchen knife."

"That was before. He's family now and whatever brought him here tonight can wait at least until the sun comes up."

Jared glanced back at Adam. "Can this wait?"

He shrugged. How in the hell did he explain why he was here?

"I need a huge favor." He gestured to his cuff. "I'll explain this in the process. But if possible, I would like to go over it only once." He shoved his hands in his pockets. "It's going to involve your whole family. I need all of you to agree—"

"Man, what the hell is going on?" Jared took a step toward him. "I've never seen you this..."

"Freaked out?" Adam slammed his fist into his pockets. "Jared, it's been a rough night. If there was any other way but to come to you, I would have taken it."

Jared relaxed his stance. "You're always welcome here. Whatever you need, just ask."

A little of Adam's tension eased from his shoulders and the base of his spine. He trusted the man in front of him with his life, with his daughter's life. But when Jared heard what Adam had to say, he knew Jared would want to eat those last words.

Understandable. The crap Adam was about to unleash on the McNeil family would wipe clean any debt they felt toward him.

"You may want to hold that thought." Adam grimaced.

"Just let me know if I need to call anyone about that," Jared replied, staring at the blood on Adam's sleeve.

"The authorities have already responded," he said in a hoarse whisper. "The murdered victim at White's Securities in DuPont Circle was my partner." Years of training slammed home and Adam stood frozen, emotionless. "The home explosion in Chevy Chase ... "

"Shit, Adam. What the hell." Jared sucked in a loud breath. "What part did you play in that? A mom and her young daughter supposedly died in that fire."

"Only the mom. They won't find the body of the little girl."

Jared's head jerked back and forth and he began to speak, but Adam interrupted.

"The little girl is my daughter, Anna. I got her out but wasn't there in time to save her mother."

"And the explosion?" Jennie asked, her voice only a whisper.

"Not me. The person responsible for setting the C-4 wanted to erase evidence of his fucking, sadistic torture of my daughter's mother. Rina, my old CIA partner, knew where to find me and she wouldn't give the bastard what he wanted fast enough. I left the scene because it's better he thinks Anna and I died in the explosion."

"Good God." Jennie covered her mouth with her hands and leaned against her husband. "Where's your daughter, Adam?"

"She's with a good friend. You know him, Robert Anthony."

"Father Anthony from St. Luke's?" Jennie and Jared asked together.

"That title always makes me cringe. My bad ass CO, a priest. It's hard to believe even after all these years. He's bringing her with him when he comes for brunch."

Jennie and Jared eyed each other. "And your favor?" Jared finally asked.

"I'm going after the bastards and I need … " He exhaled a shaky breath. "I need you to take care of Anna."

"And?" Jared's gaze never wavered from Adam's.

He knew Jared McNeil, knew he was waiting for the entire story. The rest, God, he didn't want to say it out loud.

"And raise her if I don't come back. She is a couple years younger than Emma's boys and the sweetest little girl you will ever meet."

The room grew silent, the hum of the refrigerator filling the void. Jennie was the first to find her voice.

"Of course. Like I said, you're family, but right now, you need a bed. I'm going to make up the guest room. It'll only take a couple minutes."

As she walked away, Adam reached for her arm. "The sofa is fine. Don't fuss."

"It's no bother, really." A smile touched her lips, but her eyes filled with unreleased tears.

Jared placed his arm around his wife's waist. "Adam can sleep on anything, anywhere. The sofa will be fine." He reached out to Adam, pulling him into a hug. "Get a couple hours sleep and we'll figure the rest out."

To Jared's comment, Adam could only nod. There was no figuring out anything except his plans for Anna. He turned toward the sink and rinsed out his mug. Jared flipped off the light and they left the kitchen.

At the stairwell, Jennie and Jared headed up while Adam entered the spacious living room. The large, L-shape sectional looked like heaven. He removed his jacket and draped it over the back of the sofa. He then sat and began to remove his shoes.

Jennie jogged down the stairs with her arms laden with a pillow, blanket, and one of Jared's clean dress shirts.

"I thought you could use these." She pointed with her head toward the hallway. "The second door is a full bath. Towels, an extra toothbrush can be found in the cabinet. Let me know if you need anything else."

"Thanks, Jennie." He raised the bundle. "This is very kind of you."

They both stood there, staring at each other. Her face held such expression, it wasn't hard to figure out what was going through her head.

She knows.

"Jennie, this is your home. Ask."

"How old are you, Adam?"

Her voice was so low, he almost didn't hear her. "Thirty-five next April." The answer seemed to ease the strain around her eyes.

"Thomas McNeil is a good man. He would never—"

"I know, Jennie."

Adam was four years older than Jared and his twin, Noah. As much as he wanted to give her what she needed to hear, he couldn't bring himself to say the words. He hadn't the energy to rinse and repeat his damn life over and over again.

"Okay," she said, taking in a deep breath. "So you really are his son?"

"Yes."

He could handle a yes. How he wished that one yes was enough to lift the elephant off his chest. In about three hours, somehow he was going to have to find the nerve to tell his father who he was.

A whispered *shit* escaped Jennie's lips. "And your mom?"

"She's dead. Murdered."

Jennie could only shake her head. "I'm sorry. I know how that feels. You never get over it."

"No, you don't. Any other questions?"

Her expression hardened "It didn't have to be this way, Adam."

He glanced down at his feet and then back at Jennie. "Can you keep this from Jared for a couple hours?"

She shook her head. "Jared is the one person on this earth I never keep secrets from. He's my husband." She placed a hand on his shoulder and kissed his cheek.

"Adam Blake, welcome to the family."

Chapter Seven

Ludis sprawled in a high back lounge chair and glared at a loathsome oil painting that covered the entire wall of his hotel suite. The comforter, end table, and floor were littered with blood-soaked gauze. When he couldn't stand the sight of the painting another second, he lowered his eyes and studied the doctor's handiwork. Not a sound escaped his lips as the sharp tip of the tapered needle dug into his tissue repeatedly, knotting the ragged sides of the wound together.

"Take another drink, Mr. Vasnev. This is going to hurt."

The pungent odor of antiseptic his personal physician held in his hand reeked. Ludis reached for the glass of vodka on the end table and gulped down a hefty portion of its contents. The cheap hotel bar version was bitter and burned the back of his throat but gave him the buzz he needed to deal with the pain.

"I can give you something that will take the edge off."

"No! Just get on with it." Ludis couldn't take a narcotic. He needed his wits about him.

The doctor raised a container and doused a liberal amount of the burning liquid over the deep knife wound below his shoulder.

Ludis grabbed the bottle of vodka and took another deep swig. Setting the bottle back on the table, he wiped his mouth with the back of his hand as he glared into the doctor's face.

Vodka was usually a great distraction, but not tonight. Ludis couldn't help clenching his jaw each time the doctor pressed down on the wound. The fucking knife wound was nothing. The pain from his father's blows lasted longer than this scratch.

His father, *the great Emil Vasnev*. Now that was a distraction.

Rage seethed through him, pushing the pain from his mind. He had lived daily under his father's abusive thumb and cleaned up more horseshit than he cared to track. And everything Ludis had worked so hard for the last thirty years was all about to be for nothing.

"My father … " A slight gasp of pain escaped Ludis's lips. He bit down hard on his back molars and hissed out a breath. "When was the last time you saw him?"

"Two days ago."

"And?"

A sadness edged into his doctor's eyes. "He's the same. The clinical trial had no effect reducing the cancer." The doctor removed the gauze and reached for the needle. Before he continued suturing the wound, he said, "Your father's assistant, Mr. Reese, asked me to relay a message."

The doc's eyes were glued to Ludis's chest—a sure sign of his discomfort.

"What does Reese want now?"

"He said he couldn't reach you so he wanted me to tell you time is running out. He gave me an envelope of orders from your father. I have it in my coat."

Ludis fisted his free hand. "It can go in the trash with all of this on your way out," he said, nodding at the bloodied bandages.

The man grimaced, which made him pierce the skin a little harder. Ludis bit back a groan. He didn't need to read the note to know what Reese wanted. It was another warning. If Ludis failed to deliver Adam Blake and the kid to his father before his death, the Vasnev empire would fall under Adam's control. Ludis would be left with the apartment in New York City and a few million. Petty cash.

Emil Vasnev's dying wish was to lay eyes on his daughter's only child just once.

The fucking golden child.

Ludis could still feel his father's boney fingers digging into his wrist, leaving round bruises where he clutched at Ludis's pale skin.

He actually cried, begging Ludis to bring him his only grandson. Ludis never hated his father more than he did at that moment.

Easing the cramp in his fisted hand, he faced the doctor. "How long does my father have?"

The doctor paused and met his gaze. "A month, maybe two. There is no way to know exactly. It's time to make plans."

It took everything in Ludis from shouting *thank God*. The day he buried the bastard couldn't come too soon.

What his father didn't know was that Adam Blake posed an even bigger problem than the loss of a well-deserved inheritance. His nephew's very existence was an albatross around his neck, and Adam didn't even know what he possessed.

Everything Ludis had learned about his nephew in the last several hours made one thing clear: if Blake knew about the disk, why his mother died, he wouldn't rest until Ludis was buried in the darkest pit. Since his old man was looking for some kind of heavenly forgiveness for his past sins, he wouldn't look the other way this time, but would help end Ludis's existence.

The doctor released the pressure over the wound. "I'm almost done."

He dug the needle into the top layer of skin and knotted it. Another antiseptic soaking followed.

"We should be doing this in a hospital sterile setting. I'm going to start you on a round of antibiotics. It's a deep cut and I don't want infection to set in."

"Whatever. Just hurry up."

The doctor raised his eyebrow and his lips turned into a scowl. "Mr. Vasnev, this wound isn't something to laugh about. You need to rest and give it a chance to heal or you'll pull out the stitches."

A slow burn gushed through Ludis's veins. His fisted hand begged to react, but he kept it pressed to his side while he gulped a deep breath instead. Taking his anger out on the man in front of him would serve no purpose.

"Finish closing the fucking wound, bandage it, and get the hell out."

Nothing else was said for the next several minutes as the doctor did exactly what Ludis demanded. As soon as the door clicked shut on the doctor's back, Ludis poured himself another glass of vodka and chugged half of it down like it was water. He reached over for his cell phone and punched in a number. The call was picked up on the first ring.

"Well?"

"I don't have anything for you, Mr. Vasnev. I told you I would call you—"

"Why the hell not? You have had hours to examine the remains."

The man on the other end of the phone let out a heavy sigh. "The bodies were burned beyond recognition. One female and pieces of what appear to be two males. This is going to take time."

"What about the child?"

Another heavy gasp came over the line. "Nothing yet. If she was upstairs, finding any sign of her remains will be almost impossible. The officials are combing through the wreckage. I'll call you as soon as I have anything."

Ludis's blood rushed through his veins, the throbbing so intense in the vein at his temple, he had no idea what kept the blood from bursting through his skin.

"You have one hour to get me what I'm paying you for. One hour!"

"Mr. Vasnev ... that's impossible. I can't possibly get it to you in—"

"One hour or my men have their orders. Do I make myself clear?"

Ending the call, Ludis tossed the cell on the bed and stormed into the bathroom, placing his hand under cold running water. He yanked a white hand towel off the rack, wet it, and pressed it against his face. The coolness didn't touch the fire burning within him. He raised his head and glared into the large mirror over the sink. The bandage over his left shoulder already had blood seeping through it.

If only he could have gotten to Adam's daughter. He found the safe room, but he couldn't breach Blake's security system.

How in the hell had his nephew fought through his men? It was as if he came out of the walls. One minute, they were alone with the lying bitch and the next, his two best men were dead and Blake had a knife on him.

The doorbell chimed and Ludis left the bathroom. He opened the door, letting in three men. Not one man met his gaze. He rubbed his eyes as a sinking feeling settled in the pit of his stomach.

"Your news better be more appealing than your expressions."

Each man glanced at the other. One finally spoke up.

"Sir, there is no sign of Blake." He pulled out his iPhone from his breast pocket. "We tracked his call here," he said, pointing to a cell tower off U.S.1 and the Beltway. "It's too weak a signal to pinpoint an exact location. There have been no calls since, which means he may still be in the house or—"

"*Aizpis muti!* Shut the fuck up. I want verification that Blake and the girl are either dead, or about their present location." He yanked the closest man to him. "Nothing else."

Ludis shoved the man against the wall next to the door, putting his full anger behind the move. The man grabbed his shoulder as a groan escaped his throat. A loud knock sounded and Ludis's business partner, Stefen, entered the suite. He paused for a brief moment, no doubt taking in the expressions and atmosphere in the room, and laughed. Stefan could never resist being an asshole.

"I come bearing gifts," he said, pulling out his laptop from his shoulder bag.

"You better be, Stefen. I'm ready to shoot someone." He glared at the men who lingered by the door. "Why are you morons still here?"

"Don't get rid of them just yet." Stefen lifted the computer lid. "I have men watching the brother's home. You're going to love this." He hit several keys and an infrared image came up on the monitor. "That thermal imager you procured is genius. Looky what we found."

Ludis shoved him aside to better examine the screen. "What the hell am I looking at?"

"It's an infrared image of the inside of Jared McNeil's house."

Stefen pointed at the upstairs master bedroom. The outline of the room came out in different shades of gray except for two white splotches lying on a bed in the center of the room.

Ludis shook his head. "I don't see what … "

"That image was taken at five forty-five this morning." He pointed at each of the white blobs. "We have Jared and Jennie McNeil here," he said, outlining their bodies. "But who do we have here?" He tapped another body prone on a sofa in the living room.

His gaze bored into Stefen. "Are you saying that's Blake?"

Stefen nodded. "No other people occupied the house all evening until around five when this guy showed up. And he didn't use the front door." He brought up another image. "This was taken only thirty minutes earlier." Only two people appeared on the screen. He clicked through several other photos. "McNeil's family is all accounted for. I can't think of anyone else it could be but Blake. Can you?"

Ludis glared at the monitor. "No, I can't."

A sense of triumph erupted from somewhere deep within him, but he knew no outward sign of emotion crossed his features. "And the girl?"

"There is no sign of her, but if she's alive, all we have to do is watch and wait. Blake took great pains to be part of his child's life. He won't abandon her now."

Chapter Eight

Calista leaned against the headrest and closed her eyes. Anna sat beside her in the backseat of Father Anthony's sedan, her hand clasping Calista's so tightly, her middle fingers were numb. Anna hadn't let Calista out of her sight since she woke up in the twin bed at the rectory and found Adam gone. Thankfully, Anna was comfortable around Father Anthony. She didn't fight him when he helped Calista hide her long, wavy hair under an orange Orioles's baseball cap.

Father Anthony drove into an older, well-established neighborhood of a small town west of Baltimore. After a maze of turns that Calista was too tired to make heads or tails of, he entered a cul-de-sac, parking in front of a two-story colonial. He scanned the block before he twisted in his seat.

"This is Jared and Jennie's home. Adam has worked a few cases with Jared over the years and they are good friends." With a quick smile, he unclipped his seatbelt and got out.

Anna's grip grew tighter. Calista placed her arm around Anna's shoulder and hugged her. "It's going to be okay."

A cringe sliced through her. It was such a lame thing to say, but she had to give Anna something to hold onto. There was nothing okay about the last ten hours. And trying to explain to her grandfather why she couldn't come home had been about as fun as a bat to the side of the head. How was she supposed to convince Anna of anything when all Calista wanted to do was roll into a tight ball and have a good cry?

Anna shifted and glanced out the window, her gaze on the front door. The door opened and a man stepped out on the porch and hurried down the sidewalk toward them. Fear edged into Anna's eyes as she jerked her head back and forth.

Calista leaned over and helped Anna release her seatbelt, giving the child another brief hug. Before Calista could find additional words of comfort, the door on Anna's side of the car opened.

"Hi. I'm Jared. You must be Calista." He knelt down and smiled, holding out his hand.

It was his eyes that made her stomach pitch and almost swallow her tongue. Adam's eyes stared back at her on a new yet oddly familiar face.

Where have I met this man before?

Her mind raced, searching her memories. Then it hit like a hard ball to the face how she knew Jared McNeil. He shared one of the worst moments of her life.

What were the chances that the one detective she knew, the man who interviewed her after Hanna's attack, was Adam's brother? Everything about that day, the disbelief, every horrific moment came slamming back as if it just happened. And he didn't even recognize her.

Taking his hand in hers, she said, "We've met before, Detective McNeil. I'm Hanna Tu's ... was Hanna's best friend."

Jared studied her for a moment and his tense expression softened. "Calista, I'm so sorry about Hanna. My brother Noah interviewed you and your other roommates."

"You just look so much like ..."

"Noah and I are identical twins. Most people can't tell us apart."

Calista swallowed and choked out a simple hello. He gave her a brief smile before shifting his attention to Anna. One glance at the child and his demeanor changed.

"Hi, little one." He took in a breath and let it out slowly as he studied Anna. "I'm Jared. Your dad is not here just yet, but he's on his way."

He held out his hands to help Anna out of the car, but she didn't move. Instead, her intense gaze studied his features. Jared remained perfectly still. Calista had no problem reading his expression. He knew who Anna was, and from the warmth radiating from his features, he was falling hard for the little girl.

An instant later, Anna released Calista's hand and lunged into Jared's waiting arms. He lifted her out of the car and set her onto the sidewalk. She stared up at him, and for the first time since Calista had met the child, Anna smiled—a genuine from-the-heart smile. She reached for his hand and they headed toward the front door.

Father Anthony laughed. "I guess it's true, children see things more clearly than adults. Anna knew exactly who Jared was to her." The priest peered in through Anna's side of the car. "Are you getting out?"

Calista didn't feel the sense of ease that settled over Anna. In fact, she'd never felt so uncomfortable in her life. She shoved down the sense of panic building inside her and got out of the car.

The front door opened again, pulling Calista out of her head. A petite woman with shoulder length, auburn hair waved from the porch before she moved down the sidewalk toward them. And again recognition hit hard.

"Jennie." The name came out in a breathless gasp. Calista stood motionless as an overwhelming sense of guilt slammed into her gut. Another emotion roiled right along with the guilt, but Calista couldn't quite place it.

Father Anthony joined her on the sidewalk. "You know Jennie McNeil?"

"Yes," she said, facing the priest. "Do you know who Hanna Tu is?"

He nodded as his eyes widened.

"She was my best friend. We were roommates before …"

Calista swallowed before the sob in her throat choked her.

"I had no idea, Calista," Father Anthony said, placing a hand on her arm.

"I met Jennie while visiting Hanna at the hospital and later at the rehab center. Jennie, Hanna's sister, Sarah, and I spent a lot of time together. Jennie was also targeted by that monster, but someone stopped him before he ... hurt her."

"I know."

"Sarah and I, we have always been at odds with each other. The only thing we had in common was we both loved Hanna."

My God, was Sarah here?

"I haven't been very supportive of Sarah since Hanna's death. I don't know why, but I don't even return Sarah's phone calls." So many uncomfortable emotions churned through Calista, the confession slipped out.

The priest said nothing.

"Sarah might not blame me for what happened to her sister, but I can't forgive myself for leaving Hanna in that damn apartment. That monster was just waiting for us to drive away so he could ..."

Father Anthony gently turned her to face him. "Hanna's attack isn't your fault, Calista."

"I know that here," she said, pointing to her head, "but it's just hard to believe it here." She covered her heart with the palm of her hand as her throat clogged with tears. "I was the last one to see her before the attack."

"Did you attend Sarah and Jason McNeil's wedding a few months ago?"

"No, although Sarah invited me." She faced the priest. "I was happy she found Jason. I just couldn't be there. I know it doesn't make sense, but I didn't want to spoil her day, bring everything back."

"Like you are feeling right now?"

Before she could respond, Jennie came up to her with a welcoming smile and gave her a quick hug.

"Hi, Calista. When Adam said he had a friend helping him with his daughter ... it's a small world, isn't it?"

Calista tried to return the smile, but she didn't have the skill to fake it. Instead, she reached for the passenger door. "Sorry, I don't belong here."

Adam, Hanna, Sarah, and last night—it was all coming at her too fast for her to hold onto. There was a thread here, something she was missing. As that thought sunk in, another one pushed acid into her throat. *Shit!* She was so damn naïve.

Sarah Tu was married to Adam's youngest brother, which made Sarah family. Adam had ingrained himself into Calista's world to protect his family.

"What's wrong?" Father Anthony asked.

Jennie placed a hand on her elbow. "Calista, it's okay. I know you and Sarah have some problems, but there's no need to leave. She and Jason are in Austin." She nodded toward the house and said, "It's just my in-laws and brother-in-law, Noah."

"Is Adam here?" Calista couldn't keep the tremble from her voice.

"No. He showed up around five this morning. He was gone when Jared and I came downstairs."

What the hell? "God, if he went after Ludis, I'm going to kill him."

Father Anthony stepped in front of her. "Don't jump there just yet."

She shot a glare at the priest. "He knew exactly who I was the day we met. Adam didn't just walk into my grandfather's place because he was hungry. He came to see what kind of *friend* would leave her best friend to be attacked by a serial rapist."

"Calista, I think ..."

"He worked as a spy, right? That's what the CIA does. And of course let's not discount his security business. It's his job to find people and ..."

"Calista," Father Anthony interrupted her tirade. "You have a right to demand answers, but Adam is the only one who can answer them." He paused for a brief moment then said, "Just remember one thing. Adam trusts you with his daughter. That is out of character for him. He doesn't rely on anyone for help and hasn't for as long as I have known him."

Father Anthony placed her hand in the crook of his elbow and headed toward the door. "Why don't we go inside and talk about this. I don't feel comfortable out here and I'm sure Anna is wondering where you are." His gaze scanned the neighborhood. "If you want to leave, I'll drive you someplace safe."

Anna. That was why she was here. There was no way she would leave that precious little girl hours after she lost her mother. Keeping that thought close to her heart, Calista squared her shoulders and moved toward the entrance.

Once inside, Anna ran into her arms. Calista lifted her up as she was introduced to Jared's parents, Thomas and Mary McNeil. A man almost identical to Jared took a step toward her, then stopped. He shot a glare at Jared and Jennie. Calista wasn't sure what was going on, but it made her very uneasy.

"Calista Martin, right?" he said. "What are you doing here? Maybe you don't remember me, but I …"

"Detective McNeil, of course I remember you." She tried not to stare.

"I'm Noah."

The twins stood shoulder to shoulder, examining her as if she were a bug under a microscope. Before, Noah had been so relaxed, open, even empathetic. Neither brother was approachable today. They stood on guard as if ready to attack.

Noah broke the uncomfortable silence. "Why are you here and who is this?" His expression softened when he glanced at Anna.

A door banged shut from the kitchen. Everyone turned as Adam stormed into the room.

"What the hell took you so long?" he said to Father Anthony.

"I drove the speed limit. You should try it."

Anna squirmed out of Calista's arms and raced for her father. He scooped her up, kissing her gently on the cheek, then turned his gaze to Calista. With his free hand, he reached for her but froze. "What's wrong, Calista?"

She wanted to slam a fist right smack into his sneaky, deceitful nose until she took a closer look. Adam's eyes were bloodshot and ringed with dark circles. His shirt was clean, free of Rina's blood, but his suit had that slept in, unkempt quality about it. He probably hadn't slept a wink all night.

Despite the new wariness edged into every feature, he was so damn good looking. *Miss Gullible.* That's what Pete would call her. Calista just couldn't bring herself to hit the guy when he was so down, but she had no intention of letting him off the hook. He owed her an explanation. This just wasn't the time or the place.

"Calista?"

Holding Anna against one hip, he placed his other arm around Calista's waist. His genuine concern melted a little of her resentment.

"One thing I can't stand is dishonesty. You stepped over the line and I didn't deserve that. You can be a real ass, Adam Blake."

"What?"

"I'm here for Anna. For this to work, we have to trust each other."

*

Adam could only stare at Calista. The tightness in her eyes told him unmistakably that she was pissed, really pissed, and all her anger was directed at him. What was going on inside her head?

"I told you I wouldn't leave without saying goodbye. I would never do that to Anna. Or you."

Calista's glare sliced through him. When he left her at the rectory, she was pissed at his plan for leaving Anna. This was a different kind of pissed. She was acting like he did something that really hurt her. "Look, I'll … "

"Adam, what the hell are you doing here?" Noah interrupted, taking a step closer to him. "And what's with the suit?"

"I would like to know the answer to that question myself." Thomas McNeil moved around the coffee table to stand next to Adam.

His biological father was a tall man, a good two inches over his own six-foot height. The room grew silent.

Anna touched Adam's cheek and drew his attention to her. She opened her mouth and tried to say something, but only a throaty hiss sounded. Her eyes filled with tears and she buried her head into his shoulder.

The anger in Calista's eyes evaporated. She moved closer and placed a comforting hand on Anna's shoulder.

Thomas studied him for a moment. "It's not that I'm not glad to see you, but this is a bit of a surprise. I didn't know you knew my sons."

Before he could respond, Jared interrupted.

"Dad, how do you know Adam?" Jared's stance grew rigid and his eyes narrowed.

"We've been chess partners for almost two years." Thomas glanced at his oldest son for a second. "Where did the two of you meet?"

Anna squirmed from his arms. Once her feet hit the floor, she grabbed hold of his hand and tried to pull him toward the front door.

"Sweetie, what's wrong? It's okay. You're safe here," he said, drawing her close to his side.

"And who is this little doll?" Thomas asked. Anna kept her head buried in Adam's side and her body seemed to shiver just as badly as when he lifted her out of the dresser. What had her spooked?

"Daddy, we have to leave. Now!"

Anna's words sliced through his head. The pain was so severe, his knees buckled. He leaned over and pressed his fingers into his temples.

"We shouldn't be here. Daddy, we have to go."

Adam squeezed his eyes shut as a moan escaped his throat. Seconds passed before he opened his eyes and glanced at his daughter.

"Anna, please stop." The words came out in a hoarse whisper. He swiped at the moisture sliding down the side of his face. His finger came back stained with blood.

He leaned his mouth close to his daughter's ear and tried to keep his voice quiet, but the words filled the still room. "We can't leave yet, but it's going to be okay."

His little girl shook her head back and forth. She opened her mouth and desperately tried to speak. When no sound came from her lips, she burst into silent tears. Adam moved to the sofa and cradled her in his arms. Surprisingly, Calista sat beside him and even offered him a warm smile.

Anna yanked at his collar, drawing his attention back to her. *"It's not safe here."*

The last four words were a desperate cry. Each word cut a new pathway through to the back of his skull.

"Give her what she needs, Adam," Calista pleaded.

"I can't."

Mary McNeil, who sat alone on the loveseat, reached for her husband's hand. "I think we should all sit." After everyone settled, she rose and sat down on the coffee table in front of Adam. "My husband has spoken often of you. I'm Mary."

Adam tried to offer a smile. "Thomas spoke often of you as well." He didn't know what else to say.

"I don't know if Thomas mentioned it, but I'm a doctor. What's wrong?" She pulled a couple sheets of tissue from a box on the table, swiped the blood-stained tear from his face, and studied him. "How long has this been happening?" She lifted the red-spotted tissue.

Adam cleared his throat and glanced at his watch. "First time was about twelve hours ago."

She slowly shook her head from side to side. Time seemed to stand still as she continued to stare.

She knows who I am.

Was she trying to come up with a plan to protect her family from him, or protect him from the other sons?

When she finally spoke, her voice was gentle. "You know this isn't normal." She couldn't keep the concern from her voice.

He wiped the moisture from the other side of his face and then rubbed his hand on his jeans. "Yes, ma'am, but none of this is normal."

She moved her fingers over his pulse. No one spoke as the seconds ticked away. After a minute passed, she released his hand. "What are my chances of getting you to the ER?"

He drew in a deep breath and let it out slowly. "Slim to none." His gaze scanned the room. "Anna has had a rough night and ... "

"Adam!" Calista hissed out. "A rough night? It was a hell of a lot more than a rough night."

Her angry glare shot right through him, but how was he supposed to explain what Anna had experienced in the last twelve hours? What he'd gone through? There weren't words. The life his daughter knew was gone. She lost her mother, the only constant in her life.

Calista nudged him again. "Tell them what's going on or I will."

"Or I will," Jared murmured, his eyes hard as ice.

Adam clenched his jaw and wished they'd all cease with the commands for even a few minutes. "*Can't alkta in rontfa of the idka.*"

Thomas laughed out loud. "Wow, horrid pig-Latin. Haven't heard it in years," he said, smiling at his wife. He, too, studied Adam and Calista. "If you two need a moment to talk something out, I'll be happy to entertain this young lady."

From the expression on Anna's face, something serious was going on inside his intuitive little girl's head. Anna had a channel into Adam's mind. How he wished he had one into her thoughts.

An instant later, Anna's eyes closed tight and she nodded like agreeing with someone. She then tilted her head slightly and opened her eyes. Her expression held a glazed, faraway look before it softened as if all became crystal clear. He couldn't explain Anna's strange behavior, but it made his heart pound against his chest wall.

She moved her mouth as if to speak, and again, nothing came out.

"Sweetheart, sing it." Adam's voice cracked with emotion. When she jerked her head back and forth, he hugged her. "It won't hurt. Just talk to me."

"I don't want your eyes to bleed."

Adam scanned the room. Every adult's gaze was pinned on them. Anna drew her arms around her father's shoulder and rested her head against his heart. The only sound in the room was the soft hum of the ceiling fan.

"We are not supposed to be here. We have to go, now!"

"Where are we supposed to be?"

"The bad man's coming. You have to help the nice man with the cane. If we don't hurry, it's going to be too late."

Calista tucked her hand around Adam's arm and whispered, "What is she saying?"

He had no idea how to answer. "I don't understand what she wants." His baby girl wasn't making any sense. Perhaps Mary had some training with children.

"My daughter experienced a trauma last night. She stopped talking. I don't understand what's wrong. Could you please take a look at her?"

Robert, who had remained off to the side during the whole exchange, stepped forward. "Why don't Mary and I take Anna into the kitchen for some juice and something to eat?" He held a hand out to the child. "Anna, would you like that?"

To Adam's shock, Anna nodded and scooted off his lap.

As soon as the door to the kitchen swung closed, Thomas turned to Adam, his hand balled into fists and his gaze hard. "Okay, out with it. What are you doing here? How do you know my sons, and what the hell is going on with that little girl?"

Chapter Nine

Robert had tried for years to convince Adam to tell the McNeils who he was, especially since he spent so much time with them. To Robert, an omission of the truth was nothing more than a lie and held the same consequences. Now that lie stared Adam in the face.

It was the moment he'd always dreaded.

Calista took his hand in hers and spoke in a low, hoarse voice. "No place to run, Batman. It's time … past time."

Jared shifted around Adam and dropped into a chair next to the coffee table. Noah joined his twin, his expression almost identical to Thomas's. Jennie perched on the arm of Jared's chair, her hand around his shoulder.

But Adam addressed his story to Thomas. It was Thomas's story as much as it was his and he had the right to know. "Last night, Anna's mother was murdered by a man who's after me. Rina was killed because she wouldn't give up my location. Anna was in the house."

Jared leaned on his knees. "Does this have anything to do with the home explosion in Chevy Chase?"

"Yes," he murmured. His eyes searched the door to the kitchen. "Anna's home. And since the explosion—I don't know, maybe even before—she stopped talking. She's doing this thing. I can't explain it because it's fucking crazy. I can hear her voice only in my head."

"Ah hell. Not another freak'n supernatural conversation?" Noah replied.

"I don't know how much Anna saw or heard. Calista and I found her hiding in a dresser in the safe room and got her out before the house blew."

Thomas tensed his back and shoulders. "Who did this?"

"Ludis Vasnev, my uncle. Emil Vasnev, my grandfather, controls the Vasnev syndicate in Eastern Europe."

Jared let out a groan. "Next to Ludis and Emil Vasnev, Elías Mendoza looks like a damn choir boy."

Adam watched Jared reach for Jennie's hand. "I know Mendoza brutalized you both for years, but he isn't part of this. My grandfather is a powerful man, but even he can't get to Mendoza inside the walls of a maximum security prison."

"Adam, how do you know Mendoza?" Thomas asked.

"While still with the CIA, I worked with your son Mac on a joint task force."

Thomas's features grew tense, the former police detective breaking through the father figure.

"And how are Mendoza and Vasnev connected?"

"Dad, when Mac began the special task force to take down Mendoza's organization, the Vasnev name popped up all over the place," Jared offered. "Mac and Adam tried to go after Mendoza through the Vasnev syndicate, but with every move they made against Emil Vasnev, he came out smelling like a rose."

Noah's blue eyes bore into Adam. His jaw tightened, causing the nerve in his neck to pulse. "We searched for a mole …"

"I'm no fucking mole, Noah. I spent years digging through the garbage trying to find a way to destroy my grandfather's organization."

Thomas shifted, his face distorted with anger. "What did you bring to our doorstep, Adam Blake? Why the hell are you here?"

Calista scooted closer and leaned forward slightly. "He's here to protect you."

Adam couldn't help stare at the woman next to him. When he walked into the room, Calista treated him like he was enemy number one. What changed? Hell, he couldn't remember the last time someone stood up for him without wanting something in return.

Noah shot up from the sofa. "Maybe you should leave. Anna and Calista are welcome … "

"Noah, stop!" Jared stared at his twin. "The man hasn't been straight with us, but when someone risks his life to save yours, you don't slam a door in his face when he needs help." He turned to his father. "Adam is who you can thank for my life. He's responsible for rescuing me when Mendoza was holding me prisoner." He twisted to face Noah. "And he has earned the right to ask for whatever the hell he needs. You know him. He's your friend. After what he's done for us, how can you turn your back on him?"

"Just give him a chance to explain," Calista whispered.

Adam could have sworn she was ready to cry. He stood and took several steps away from the group, needing space to think. "If I could have kept you out of this nightmare, I would have."

"If Vasnev is as bad as you and my son suggest," Thomas paused, looking between Adam and Jared, "and he's after you, how is coming into my son's home going to protect any of us?"

"I came to warn you and convince you to move into a safe house I arranged for your family." Adam eyed the group. "Ludis used Rina to get information about me. He went after her and my daughter, my business partner, my adopted family."

"Sorry, Adam. Warn us of what exactly?" Thomas asked.

Adam's throat closed up on him and acid burned the thin wall of his stomach. Only Calista's expression, raised eyebrows and a slow, deliberate blink that all but dared him not to chicken out, strengthened his resolve. He'd give her one thing—she knew how to hang tough under pressure.

"I'm Annija's son." He slipped his hand into the inside pocket of his sport coat and pulled out a dog-eared photo. "Do you remember her?"

Thomas reached for the photo. After a quick glance, he stood with his back ramrod straight while he tried to regain his breath. "Yes, I remember Annija. She is … unforgettable." He pulled his gaze away from the photo and studied Adam. "Is that you with her in the picture?"

Adam could only nod.

"I met her while on leave in Rome thirty-six years ago. I haven't seen her since. She disappeared out of my life."

Adam took the photo. "She didn't disappear. She was grabbed off the street in front of the bakery down from the hotel where the two of you were staying."

"By whom?" Thomas asked.

"Emil Vasnev, her father. He sent his men after her. Several weeks later, she discovered she was pregnant."

"I looked everywhere for her for months."

"She was protecting you." Adam's words came out in a forced, throaty whisper.

Noah let out a string of curse words, but no other sound came from any of the family members. Adam lowered his head and rubbed the back of his neck.

"Adam, it's okay. Just get it out."

Calista's voice was quiet, but firm, almost encouraging. It was as if she was on his side, giving him what he needed to get through it. When he glanced at her, she lifted her head and met his gaze with such warmth, he had to swallow the lump that formed in his throat before he could speak.

"At the first opportunity, she escaped from Emil's compound in Latvia. She knew how to disappear; her father taught her well how to go underground. She hid until a year after I was born. She found my adoptive parents … gave me up, and went back to her father alone. She'd rather protect me from her father than have me raised under Emil's roof. From what she wrote in her diaries, she hated what her father did for a living." He took in another deep breath, but his lungs were still airless. "She didn't reach out to you because she knew you would never walk away and her father would have you killed."

Restless, he began pacing until he backed up so far, his back hit the wall. Calista eased next to him and threw an arm around his waist, drawing his weight to her. He didn't understand why, but he could explore that later. Right now he needed her strength.

No one moved. Thomas broke the silence. "Finish it, Adam."

Adam settled his stance. "It took Emil almost eighteen years to discover me. I imagine it was a total betrayal in his eyes. He must have sent Ludis after me. My uncle found my adopted parents alone in our home. I was at school." He stared at his birth father, trying to find the next words. "Annija intercepted me on my way home and sent me into hiding. Ludis killed her for it."

"His own sister?" Thomas closed his eyes.

"How do you know Vasnev killed your birth mother?" Noah asked.

"I watched him ram her car off the road into a canyon. It exploded on impact."

Noah raked a hand over his face then said, "There is nothing about Ludis Vasnev wanted for murder in the United States. You never reported this, called the police, or ..."

"I was a kid, Noah, a stupid, scared kid. And I had no idea who the bastard was. Annija told me to run ... and I saw what he did to my parents. By the time I figured out the right thing to do, Ludis was gone and my parents, Annija — everyone I loved was gone."

Calista moved her hand up Adam's arm and hugged him. Adam sure the hell didn't earn this support but he wasn't going to turn it down either. He reached for her hand and held it in his.

"I used the new identity Annija created for me and joined the Marines. I wanted the training to go up against the bastard who killed my family." Adam turned and shot a glare at Noah. "I don't know why Ludis went to such brutal extremes to kill his sister. What he got in return was a fucking thorn in the Vasnev organization."

"Adam, when did you discover who Ludis Vasnev was?" Thomas's eyes glistened with unshed tears. He knew the answer to his question, but Adam was aware that Thomas needed to hear the words said out loud.

"After several tours in the Middle East, the CIA recruited me and partnered me with Rina Russo."

The memory of the first day he and Rina walked into that multi-agency task force flashed before him. "The Vasnevs had connections to known terrorist groups in the Middle East, and I knew the area well. We were assigned to work with Mac's task force. Ludis Vasnev's ugly mug shot and photos of his vicious handywork for the last five years were spread out on the conference table during our first briefing." Adam swallowed hard. "I had been searching for him for years, and Mac handed him to me on a silver platter."

"Shit, Adam. I was in that briefing," Jared said. "We met that day after I briefed the group on Mendoza. You said nothing ..."

"What the hell did you expect me to say, Jared? I spent the next few days connecting the dots. If I revealed my connection to you, I would have been removed from the task force. That wasn't happening." He shot a hard stare at Noah. "Not because I was protecting them, but because I wanted to be the one who took them down." He released Calista's hand and raked his fingers through his hair. "At least that was the plan until..."

"Until Anna." Thomas murmured.

"Yes, everything went to hell when Rina got pregnant with Anna." Adam paused and took in a deep breath. "Rina was the only person I trusted. I told her about my Vasnev family connection and we both dived into a relentless campaign to destroy the bastard's empire. Our lives didn't leave much room for any type of relationship from the outside, so Rina and I became more than just partners. When she gave birth to Anna, we went undercover, so to speak, to keep our daughter's life a secret."

Calista eased a little closer and brought her other hand and pressed it over his. The simple gesture had such strength behind it.

"And now Vasnev has discovered Anna?" Jared asked, the tension in his face very easy to read.

"Yes."

"And he's also discovered who fathered you." Jared's voice came out hoarsely.

Adam met his father's uncompromising stare. "You're my father, sir. He's coming after you because you're the only one left to leverage against me."

"Why is Vasnev coming after you so strongly now? What does he want from you?" Jared asked.

"I have no idea."

The kitchen door eased open and Father Anthony stood in the doorway. "See, that wasn't so hard."

If his friend weren't wearing a collar, Adam would almost be tempted to give him a nosebleed. The priest just chuckled, took a bite of his sweet roll, and went back into the kitchen.

Noah took an angry step toward Adam, his stance rigid. "You have known you were a McNeil, my damn brother, from the beginning, and you said nothing all these years."

Thomas glanced at his sons and motioned for them to sit. He turned slowly to Adam, his eyes watering. "So you are here because he has also discovered me, my family… your family."

"Yes."

"And you're worried he will come after us like he went after Anna's mother?"

"Yes."

Mary came through the kitchen door and approached her husband. She drew him back to the sofa. "Thomas, sit. Your heart."

"Is Anna okay?" Adam asked.

"Yes, Father Anthony is entertaining her."

Adam took a tentative step toward his father. "What's wrong with his heart, Dr. McNeil?"

"Adam, I think under the circumstances, you should at the very least call me Mary." She pushed on her husband's shoulders and he sat. "I'm sure you have your reasons for this game you have been playing with all of us."

"It wasn't a game."

"Sorry. Bad choice of words." Mary approached him and placed her hand on his lower back and led him and Calista to the empty loveseat. "Sit." She glanced at her sons, then settled down next to her husband. "We all need to deal with this." Her gaze met Adam's. "What I meant to say is that I'm sure you kept your identity from us for your own reasons. We can hash that out later, but for now, what is the immediate threat?"

"Ludis Vasnev is very dangerous and his resources extend beyond anything you can imagine. By now, he knows everything about you, your likes, dislikes, routine … everything."

Jared shifted, his fist clenching and unclenching on his knee. "So how do we protect ourselves?"

"You can't. You will never see him coming." Adam pressed Calista's hand gently and released it. "But you don't have to worry about Ludis. I will stop him. I'm here because I have no one to leave Anna with."

The next instant, a sharp, piercing pain shot from behind his eyes to the back of his head. He dropped to his knees and covered his head with his hands, an agonizing moan escaping deep within him. Anna's voice tore through his head, leaving behind a pounding headache.

"Daddy, you can't leave me here." Anna raced through the kitchen door to her father.

"Anna, stop it!" Adam pleaded through the pain. He wrapped his arms around her.

"Daddy, you can't leave. You will die, too, like Mommy."

He lifted her chin. "Baby girl, calm down. You're hurting me."

Mary moved toward them and placed her hand on his child's shaking shoulders to lead her away. "Anna, come sit with your grandpa." Thomas immediately cradled Anna when Mary set her on his lap.

The pain lessoned and Adam dabbed at the blood seeping from the corner of his eyes. Mary helped him stand and eased him back to the loveseat. "Jennie, get my bag."

Jennie darted to the front door and retrieved a large multi-colored canvas bag for her mother-in-law. Mary unzipped the top and removed what look like a midsize travel make-up pouch. She untied the ribbon and opened it on the coffee table. She removed a small flashlight and shined the light into the back of Adam's eye.

"Dr. McNeil, I'm fine. Don't fuss. The pain is easing."

"No, Adam, you're not fine. Now be still." She took hold of his chin and flashed the light back and forth across his eyes. Her touch was gentle, her expression was anything but. "How many of these episodes have you had?"

"Four ... no five." He lowered his voice so Anna wouldn't hear, which was stupid since his daughter was probably reading his mind.

"They started when Anna began speaking to me by ..."

"Telepathy?"

"Yes. God, that sounds crazy."

This time Mary's face brightened with the first real smile since she'd walked back into the room. "Not in this group, it doesn't. We've had some unusual hands-on experience with telepathy."

"Then I'm not going crazy?"

"No, just carrying on a new family tradition."

After taking his pulse and listening to his heart, she removed a portable blood pressure machine and wrapped the large cuff around his upper arm. "Your pulse is a little fast, but the rest of your vitals are fine. But you need to see a friend of mind at Hopkins."

"It's going to have to wait."

"This is serious, Adam."

"I'm working within a very small window. I have to stop Ludis before he makes his move on you. I don't have time …"

"What the hell do you mean you have to stop Ludis?" Thomas's voice was laced with authority. "You're *not* going after him without backup."

Adam straightened his spine. "Yes sir, I am. This is my fight. I'll end it."

"Like hell you will." Thomas darted from his seat, seeming to forget he held his granddaughter in his arms.

"Thomas, the child," Mary said at his side.

But Anna was already flying to Adam, then frantically patting his face. He was afraid she was on the verge of a stroke, so jerky were her movements. "Sing the words, Anna," came Calista's soft suggestion.

His daughter nodded but didn't attempt to speak. No one said a word while Anna's voice sang inside his head.

"I have to go with you. I have to."

"Anna, this is your family," he explained, his hand extending to everyone in the room. Pray God they would accept his daughter even if they never trusted him again. "You have grandparents, aunts, uncles, and cousins your age. You won't be alone."

The little girl shook her head back and forth. "*The white hair monster will hurt you. Listen!*"

Adam's heart dropped to his stomach. God, she's seen Ludis.

Calista's hand gripped his elbow. "Someone's here."

Adam turned toward her. Her widened eyes were on the living room window.

"What?"

"Someone just drove up in a black Lincoln limo." The tremble was back in her voice. "Do you know this man?"

Adam placed Anna back in his father's lap and moved toward the window. He eased the sheers away and studied the well-dressed gentleman strolling up the sidewalk.

"What the hell?"

Emil Vasnev's associate strolled up the sidewalk like he owned the place. Charles Reese had managed Emil's legal operations for the last twenty years, and just because Adam could never find anything on the sidekick to connect him to his grandfather's other enterprises didn't mean he wasn't as guilty as everyone else in the operation.

Adam yanked his revolver from the holster inside his coat. Charging to the front door, he pulled it open, steadied his stance, and aimed the gun at the man's heart.

"One more step and I'll drop you where you stand, Mr. Reese."

From the corner of his eye, Adam could see that Jared and Noah stepped out onto the porch, their weapons at their sides. His brothers may have wanted nothing more than to use Adam's face as a punching bag, but now, when he needed their support, he got it without question.

The elegantly dressed man paused with his foot on the bottom step of the porch. His posture stiffened. He studied Adam with a pinched, almost bored expression. "Adam, you have nothing to fear from me. Stop pointing that damn weapon in my face." He reached into his jacket.

"Don't."

"I'm here to deliver a message from your grandfather."

Chapter Ten

Adam hesitated for a moment then held his weapon to his side. He took the letter and turned to Jared. Lowering his voice, he said, "Get Anna into the kitchen with Robert."

"Done."

Adam approached Reese. "You're not carrying a weapon into this home. Hand it over."

"I'm not carrying a weapon."

When Adam let out a loud grunt, Reese raised his hands above his head. "Pat me down if you don't believe me."

Adam gave him a quick pat down and then stepped to the side. "Inside."

Reese nodded, but before he took another step, he scanned the yard.

"What's wrong?" Adam asked.

The older gentleman shook his head dismissively and entered the home. The living room was dead silent. No one spoke, each member of the McNeil family assessing the stranger.

Thomas stood and broke the silence. "Mr. Reese, what business do you have with Adam?"

"I'm here to fulfill a dying man's last wish."

The man was looking about the room like he was searching for something.

"What are you looking for?" Adam hissed.

Reese smiled and took a step further into the room. "I was hoping to meet Anna. She looks so much like Annija and I wished to tell Emil …"

Adam saw red. "I don't give a fuck what pleases Emil Vasnev. He can rot until hell comes and drags his body away. He's never coming anywhere near my daughter." Before he could register his actions, he had his gun back in his hands, leveled at the snake of a messenger's head.

Reese didn't react, nor did his eyes waver from the barrel even to blink. In a sudden move that completely surprised Adam, the man struck out to grip Adam's wrist with his left hand. For a man twenty years his senior, Reese's hold was strong and the pressure of his fingers would leave bruises on Adam's wrist.

"Lower your weapon, Adam," he said calmly. "You may not want your grandfather's help, but he is the only one who can protect you from Ludis."

Keeping his weapon steadily pointed at the man's head, Adam said, "I'll take my chances."

As soon as the words were out of his mouth, Anna's voice yelled inside his head.

"He's not a bad man, Daddy. Read the letter."

A sharp pain spread through his frontal lobe. He swayed, then found his balance. A moan escaped before Adam could stop it and he rubbed his temples.

How was she doing this? Robert wouldn't allow Anna anywhere near the door. How did she see the damn letter? See Reese?

Adam rolled his neck and took in a breath to ease the stabbing pain. Reese hadn't moved an inch, but studied him with concern in his eyes.

"Are you willing to jeopardize your daughter's life or," his eyes scanned the room, "your family's life because of a horrible misunderstanding?"

"What fucking misunderstanding? That Emil ordered his own son to murder my mother or that he ordered Rina's execution?"

"Emil Vasnev may have his sins, but killing a family member isn't one of them, especially Annija. Your mother was the only good thing that Emil feels he has ever done. I was with him when the news came in about her death." Reese wiped a hand over his forehead. "It destroyed him. He was rotting away until he discovered you. A part of his Annija lives in you. He's been trying to protect you for years even though you haven't made it very easy. All he wants is to keep you safe, keep your daughter safe."

"That's bullshit."

A hand landed on Adam's left shoulder and Thomas leaned close to his ear. "Maybe you should read the letter. See what the man has to say."

Thomas's expression was one Adam never expected from the man he had lied to for two years: Concern. And with that concern came trust. Thomas trusted him to do the right thing.

Adam lowered his weapon and tore open the envelope, unfolding a sheet of white stationery. Several photos were tucked inside the fold. He flipped through one, then another, and his heart slammed against his rib cage.

The photos spanned several years. The first photo was of him and Rina having drinks in a Turkish bar in Istanbul. He remembered that mission, or at least the days after it, with such clarity. Those drinks led to the most amazing three days with Rina. They made Anna that weekend.

Before he could drift further into memories he didn't have the strength to revisit, he placed the photo in the back of the pile. The next two photos were taken after he faked his own death. He ground his molars at images of Anna hours after her birth and a year later playing in a small swimming pool in her back yard. The last photo was taken only a couple weeks ago. He was seated in his normal booth at Pete's diner, laughing at something Calista had said while she poured him a refill of coffee.

Adam handed his father the photos to read the short note written in a bold, but shaky script:

All I have ever wanted was your safety. Couldn't save Annija. Allow me to help. Ludis

must be stopped and I'm the only one he fears.
—Emil Vasnev

Reese took a step into his personal space. "If Emil Vasnev wanted you brought to him, he could have done so at any time. He knows you want nothing to do with him. Annija went to great extremes to keep you away from him. He has tried to respect her wishes, but all that has changed. Ludis will stop at nothing to see you and Anna dead."

"Why should I trust you ... trust this man?" he said, crumpling the sheet of paper in his fist.

"Your uncle wants Emil's empire. If Emil dies without a direct heir, everything will go to Ludis because there is no proof you exist."

"Ludis is Emil's son." Adam raked an angry hand over his face. "He can have it all. I don't want anything from—"

"Adam, you can't be this shortsighted." Reese's eyes narrowed and his lips pressed together in a slight grimace. He studied Adam for several moments, then glanced down at the watch on his wrist before he spoke. "You are aware that Emil isn't Ludis father, right?"

"No. What are you talking about?"

"Emil never remarried after Annija's mother died in childbirth. Instead, he went through a string of mistresses, one of them sharing a nasty little disease—turning him sterile." Reese shoved a hand in his pocket. "Emil never was good at sharing. If he had known that Ludis's mother took in another man while still with him, he would have put a bullet in her head. When she showed up pregnant and claimed the kid was Emil's, he moved her into the estate. After the birth, she disappeared. A paternity test proved what Emil already suspected. He set up a private adoption of Ludis, claiming him as his own. But he isn't a true Vasnev."

Reese checked his watch again, a sure sign of agitation. Maybe he was just uncomfortable about sharing Emil's secrets. Whatever had the man so wound up was making Adam nervous as hell. Too many pieces of the puzzle just didn't fit. "Why doesn't he change his will and give the damn money away?"

Thomas cleared his throat. "Adam, donating all his wealth would be a litigation nightmare."

"If you don't meet with your grandfather and claim your birthright, Emil's entire fortune—his name, power, everything he amassed over the last five decades—will go to your sadistic bastard of an uncle." The muscle in Reese's jaw flexed and he placed his hands on his hips. "And you, Anna, and your family will never be safe," he added. "You're in the way of what Ludis has craved his whole life: the power of the Vasnev empire."

Jared took two angry steps toward Reese. "You expect Adam to just trust you? Where the hell were you last night?"

"Daddy, the white-haired man is almost here."

Anna's words struck the back of Adam's head like a fiery poker. The door of the kitchen opened and she ran to Adam. There was almost no color in her cheeks and she clung to his leg as if her life depended on it. She reached out to him. He handed his weapon to Jared and drew her into his arms. Her arms circled his neck as her body trembled. He placed a hand over the back of her head, rocking her back and forth. "I got you, sweetheart. No one will hurt you."

She raised her head and placed her hand on his cheek. *"Run."*

Adam turned and glared at Reese. "Where is Ludis?"

Before he could answer, a small buzz sounded from inside Reese's sport coat pocket. He removed his cell phone and read the text message. "You have less than five minutes to make up your mind. Emil has a man working for Ludis and he knows you're here … that Anna is here."

"How?"

"You just said it. He has unlimited resources."

Father Anthony, who stood off by himself during most of the exchange, stepped forward. "I'll travel with you and Anna to do what I can."

Adam shook his head. "That's not your life anymore, Robert. I can't ask you to—"

"You're not asking." He turned to Thomas. "You need to get everyone out of here."

"I can protect my family," Thomas said, placing an arm around his wife's shoulder.

"No, Mr. McNeil, you can't," Reese said firmly. "Ludis isn't coming alone, so my men will escort your family to a safe place."

"No," Adam yelled. "I have made arrangements for my father's family."

"Regardless, they will be under the protection of Emil Vasnev. If we are going to move, we have to move now. Decide."

Chapter Eleven

Calista hadn't been able to fill her lungs with a good breath of air since she left Jared McNeil's home three hours ago. The flight to upstate New York in Emil Vasnev's private jet had passed in a daze, with Anna sleeping in her lap, refusing to release her almost chokehold around Calista's neck. The moment they exited the plane at a private airport near Lake Placid, they were ushered into an SUV.

Calista assumed they were heading toward an upscale hospital. Instead, they arrived at a massive estate nestled in thick, forest-covered hills. The grounds blended into the landscape. What took Calista's breath away were the spacious foyer, grand staircase, and plush living room waiting behind the home's massive double oak doors. Why would a man like Emil Vasnev surround himself with such calming beauty?

"When did my grandfather move here? He hadn't left Latvia in thirty years."

Thick, oppressive tension rolled off Adam standing behind her in waves, to the point she wanted to jump right out of her own skin. His entire demeanor slowly dissolved the closer they got to his grandfather. This man wasn't the Adam Blake she'd seen in the past 36 hours. This was the cold, distant machine who had killed two of Ludis's operatives barehanded in Chevy Chase.

"Your grandfather moved here for an experimental cancer trial. So far, the treatment hasn't been successful. We plan to return home in a few weeks."

Calista had no problem reading between the lines. Emil Vasnev moved halfway around the world for one last chance to live. He was returning home to die. The thought, for some reason, saddened her.

Adam's expression spoke volumes. He didn't care. When his gaze met hers, he didn't particularly display warm, fuzzy feelings toward her either. She knew he didn't want her there, but how did he just turn off his emotions like that?

"Let me take her," Adam said, reaching for Anna in her arms.

Instead, Anna hugged Calista closer. At least Anna wanted her. She tried to set the girl down, but she immediately wrapped her legs tighter around Calista's waist and hung on. What did this four-year-old know that the rest of them didn't? And then Calista's pulse began to race. What if Anna knew her father would soon need both hands free?

"It's okay. I got her." Calista shifted to face Adam. There was no sign of pain at this rejection in his eyes—just pure, unreleased anger.

Calista glanced back at Father Anthony. His expression wasn't any better. The priest collar was a stark contradiction to the man at Adam's right. It was as if he was readying for the battle of his life.

Reese spoke to one of the armed guards in the archway leading to the formal living room before addressing Adam. "If you would like to freshen up, I have rooms prepared for your stay."

Adam shook his head. "Let's get this over with."

He moved in close behind Calista. The heat of his breath caressed her neck. She resisted the urge to try to break the ice between them. He may not want her there, but she was going to do everything in her power to keep Anna safe. His safety was his own concern, she thought peevishly.

As if Adam could read her thoughts, he placed his hand on her lower back and leaned in close to her ear. "Do exactly what I tell you, understand? If I say run, then run with Anna like hell. Get out anyway you can."

His voice was hard, unfeeling, but when Calista glanced over at him, the fear in his eyes shocked her to her core. She nodded and let out a shaky breath, somehow placing one foot in front of the other to climb the stairs.

The second floor branched off into three separate wings. Reese lightly knocked and entered a large sitting room without waiting for an answer.

Calista took a step into the room, but Adam yanked her back against him and moved in front of her. Father Anthony remained behind. When she looked back to find him he tried to smile, but it came up short. He was wound as tightly as Adam.

What kind of man was Emil Vasnev to produce this fear in men like Adam and Father Anthony?

The downstairs was plush, but this room was simple in its elegance. The dusty blue tufted sofa sat center flanked by soft, green lounge chairs against jeweled tone walls. A large bouquet of mixed summer blooms was placed on the oak coffee table. The most striking piece of furniture was a mini-grand piano in an alcove near one of the three floor-to-ceiling windows. Calista's eyes roamed from the breathtaking artwork that hung on the walls to the lush Oriental rugs. It was the most beautiful space she had ever seen.

It took her a moment to notice the older gentleman, leaning his weight on a cane as he stood behind the piano, his back against the window. Emil Vasnev.

He held himself completely still, his physique so much like Adam's, just a little over six feet tall with broad shoulders. His hair was white and he wore it long over the collar of his dress shirt. He reminded Calista of an intense James Brolin. But the signs of cancer were evident in the dark shadows around his eyes and the hollow and sunken cheeks. At that moment, his dark brown eyes studied Adam with the same intensity Adam studied him.

Her attention was so drawn to Emil, she forgot she held Anna until the child squirmed to be let down. As soon as Anna's feet hit the floor, she took a step away from Calista. Anna also studied her great-grandfather, but unlike her father, a slight smile appeared at the corner of her lips. She took another step toward him. Calista placed her hand on the girl's shoulder, drawing her back against her. But Anna wasn't going to be held back. She shook Calista's hand off and took one step, then two, and finally ran across the room before anyone could stop her.

"Anna!" Adam cried out. He reached inside his coat and pulled out his Glock.

Father Anthony placed his hand over Adam's. "Don't."

Adam gestured to his daughter. "Anna, come here. Now!"

Anna didn't even look back at her father. She eased around the piano and stood inches from her great-grandfather, never taking her eyes off him.

"I mean it, Anna. Come here." Adam's voice came out hard, unyielding.

It only took a split second and Anna went into Emil's arms. He lifted her up and held her close against his chest. The two clung to each other like they were long-lost friends.

Adam froze, and nothing moved except the pulsing vein in his forehead. Calista could almost hear the enamel on his teeth grinding. He shoved his gun back in the holster and took two angry steps toward the center of the room. Calista didn't understand why she did it, but she reached out for his elbow, and pulled him back to her. When his fierce gaze met hers, she stood her ground.

"Look at them, Adam. He's not going to hurt her."

Emil glanced up and took a couple unsteady steps toward Adam. "She is beautiful, looks just like my Annija did at this age."

Adam said nothing in reply, but his fingers kneaded his temples.

Calista leaned closer to his ear and whispered, "What is she saying?"

"Be nice," he forced out through clenched teeth.

Emil approached his grandson and held out his hand. "I've dreamed of this moment for a long time. It's a pleasure to finally meet you."

Adam didn't lift his hand. A heavy, uncomfortable tension filled the room. Calista struggled with how to defuse the moment. Before she could react, Adam took the choice from her hands.

"Give me my daughter." His irises grew dark, almost black, and dead cold. The next instant, a tortured moan escaped from the back of his throat, and he bent at the waist, clutching his head. Calista shot a look at Anna and shook her head. She then reached for Adam's arm and led him to the sofa. When he raised his head, bloody tears streamed down his cheeks.

Emil sucked in a heavy breath. "Good God, what's wrong?" He frantically sought Reese. "Get the doctor in here now."

Adam raised his hand. "I don't need a damn doctor." He shot up from the sofa and took another angry step toward his grandfather. "Give me Anna."

Emil hugged the child in his arms and said, "I really enjoyed meeting you, little one." He then removed her small arms from around his neck and handed her over to Adam. When he spoke, his voice was heavy with emotion.

"I would never allow anything to harm her ... or you." He stepped back and dropped onto the sofa as if he couldn't stand another minute. He probably couldn't.

Calista almost reached out to help support Adam's grandfather, but pinned her hands together behind her instead. For whatever happened or didn't happen, Emil Vasnev had caused Adam immeasurable pain and she couldn't let that thought go no matter how caring he appeared holding Anna.

Reese quickly offered him a hand, but he brushed it off.

"I'm not an invalid," he snapped before giving Adam his full attention. "You are safe here. One of my men planted with Ludis texted his last location, but Ludis was gone before my team could react. I'm honored you allowed me to meet Anna. Reese has arranged rooms for you and your friends in another wing."

Calista heard the dismissal loud and clear. Emil Vasnev wasn't the man she thought he would be, but then again, neither was Adam. There was such joy in Emil's expression when Anna raised her arms for him to pick her up. And there was obvious concern when Emil saw the blood on Adam's cheek. But it was the pain and then acceptance that edged into his features when he handed Anna back to Adam that tore at her heart.

But she needed to trust Adam, trust his instincts. It was what she expected of him. Adam knew this man, studied him, and learned everything he could about his world. Calista would be crazy not to follow his lead and give in even an inch. "Maybe we should allow Anna to rest. I'll stay with her," she offered.

This time Adam did look her in the eye. "We leave together."

"Adam, Father Anthony can come with me. You need to … "

"I have nothing to say." He placed his hand at her waist, and with a not so gentle shove, pushed her toward the door.

Reese opened the door for them. His eyes, too, were hard, cold. "If you need anything, just ask." When Adam passed through the doorway, Reese said in a forced hiss, "You're making a mistake. There is little time to—"

Emil cleared his throat. "It's okay, Charles. Let him go. I have what I need."

Those five words did something to Adam. The little control he held onto his anger broke. "What the fuck does that mean?"

When Emil didn't answer, Adam yanked out his weapon and charged back into the room, stopping inches from his grandfather. He lifted his gun and aimed it at the old man's chest.

Emil stood, shifted his body until he was square with the Glock. "Go ahead. Shoot. No one here will stop you."

Chapter Twelve

Adam's pulsed drummed between his ears. "Answer my question, old man. What did you mean you have everything you need?"

Reese silently appeared at his side with his own gun inches from Adam's head. "Lower your weapon, Adam."

Emil's guards seemed to grow out of the woodwork. From the corner of his eye, he counted three more men aiming at him.

"Daddy. Stop. Don't."

This pain was much more severe than the others. He tried to find his balance, but he stumbled, reaching out for an armchair to steady himself.

Emil took a step forward and raised his hand. "Charles, leave us."

"Sir, I … "

"You heard me. Leave us."

It took a moment, but Reese and the guards backed away, moving down the hallway out of sight. Without taking his gaze off his grandfather, Adam said, "Answer my question. I won't ask again."

"Adam, give him a chance to explain," Calista said calmly and placed a hand at his waist.

Hell, he'd forgotten she was still in the room. He kept expecting Calista to run for the hills, but at every turn, she stood right next to him, not giving an inch, even to him. Rina was like that once.

Emil's body gave a slight tremble before he leaned his hand against the back of the lounge chair for support. His hand dropped to his side and his shoulders sagged as a lone tear slipped down his cheek, dropping onto the collar of his dress shirt.

That simple sign of emotion touched something deep inside Adam. He lowered his gun to his side but didn't set the safety in place. So many conflicts stirred through him he didn't know how to process them. For sixteen years, he hated everything to do with Emil Vasnev. He was the enemy, a murderer. He ordered his own daughter's execution.

Or did he? Could it all have been Ludis?

Rina had kept Anna protected, isolated, and reinforced a natural fear of strangers. As a result, Anna allowed very few close to her. But with her great-grandfather, she raced across the room and into his arms. There was such joy in his little girl's face when they embraced. How in the hell did that make any sense?

Adam swallowed a lump so he could breathe. The man in front of him may have once been a ruthless bastard, but had the man Adam Blake allowed himself to become have any right to stand there and judge Emil Vasnev? The image of Rina's lifeless body flashed before his eyes. Adam had his own sins he would never be able to right.

His grandfather cleared his throat. "I didn't send Reese for you as some kind a trick to get you and Anna under my roof."

"Then explain."

Emil slumped into the lounge chair. "My only wish was to see you just once with my own eyes. Meeting Anna, holding her in my arms is more than I could have ever wished for." His gaze met Adam's. "That's all I meant."

A hand stroked the swell of Adam's spine. Calista's hand moved down his arm to his wrist. "Adam, put it away."

The grip of his gun grew moist from sweat. After what felt like minutes but could have only been ten seconds, he abruptly clicked the safety in place and set the weapon in its holder. He instinctively glanced at Calista. She was still there, again standing by his daughter like Anna's own personal guardian angel.

The man Adam hated, even feared, wasn't the Emil Vasnev slumped in the chair. Did that man even exist today?

A sheen of sweat covered Emil's forehead. He reached into his coat pocket and removed a small, plastic pill bottle. Holding the bottle in one hand, he used his palm to loosen the lid. After several tries, he dropped his arm as if it were too heavy to hold up. The bottle landed in his lap and Emil stared into space.

Adam approached his grandfather. He knelt, picked up the bottle, and removed the lid, shaking out a small, white, oval tablet. He placed the pill in his grandfather's palm. Emil popped the pill in his mouth and swallowed. Adam turned the bottle in his hand. There was nothing identifying the medicine.

"What did you just take?"

It took a moment for Emil to answer. "It's an experimental drug for chronic pain."

"How long does it take to work?" Adam kept his hand on his grandfather's arm. A rapid beat pulsed underneath his fingers.

"Charles tried to get me to take it an hour ago, but it sometimes makes me very tired. I didn't want to miss your arrival."

Adam rose and reached for the glass of water sitting on a crystal coaster. "Can I get you anything?" he said woodenly.

Emil's eyes shone. "No, thank you. It's fast acting. The pain is already easing some," he said, patting Adam's arm.

Both men studied each other for a long time. Emil finally broke the standoff. "You have questions. Ask them."

Adam didn't even know where to start. He pulled over the footstool next to his grandfather and sat. "You are not going to like my questions."

"No, but it's time you knew who you are."

"I know who I am."

Emil exhaled a noisy sigh. "Ask what you want, Adam."

"Did you order my mother's execution?"

"No! God no. Annija was my life, my joy. I adored your mother, lived for her. The man you hate died the day she died."

He grabbed Adam's arm. "How could you think that?" The words seemed to clog in his throat. "My daughter's car went over a cliff."

"Your son rammed her car into that guardrail."

"No. That's impossible. Ludis would never ..." Emil placed his hand over his chest. His face drained of all color and his breathing hitched.

"I watched the whole fucking thing from the trees above the turn."

"Tell me! I want to know everything you witnessed."

"Annija was waiting for me outside my school. We drove into the hills toward home. When we turned onto my street, there was a car in the driveway and two men stood guard by the door. Ludis exited the house. I had no idea what was happening ... what he just did to my parents." The memory churned like acid in the pit of his stomach. "Annija sped out of the neighborhood. She pulled over onto the shoulder of the road in front of a hiking trail that led up into the hills. She told me my uncle just killed my parents and I was next. Everything else I needed to know was in a backpack she shoved out the window before she drove away."

Adam rubbed a hand across the back of his neck and swallowed a lump of grief and anger. "The path came out at the edge of the road high above the turn. I watched your son," he shot Emil with a glare, "slam into the back of Annija's car and push her over that ridge. The car exploded on impact. Ludis charged down the hill. At first, I thought he was trying to save her, but instead of pulling her from the burning car, he just stood there and watched it burn."

Emil ran a hand across his face as his eyes filled with tears. "All these years you thought I was responsible?"

Adam couldn't speak. His heart crashed against his chest. The best he could do was nod.

"No wonder you hate me." Emil didn't say anything for a long time. "I have sinned in this life and I'll pay dearly for those sins, but killing my daughter isn't one of them. Ludis will pay." His eyes grew dark, hard, and for the first time since Adam walked into the room, he knew he was seeing the real Emil Vasnev.

"She was the best of me. Hurting Annija would be inflicting pain on myself."

Adam didn't know why it mattered, but for some reason, that fact alone eased his heart enough that he could breathe again. "Did you send Ludis after me that day?"

"I didn't even know you existed until a month after Annija's death." Emil fisted his hands and winced. Pain edged in his features and he clamped down on his jaw as he stared into space.

"If the pain is too bad, we can do this later."

"No, it's been too long already." He removed a white, crisp handkerchief from the inside of his coat pocket and patted his forehead. "I was missing your mother and went into her room. It was exactly as she left it—the only thing I had left of her." A tear escaped the corner of his eye. "I chose one of her favorite books from the bookshelf and your picture fell out. One look and I knew."

"Knew what?"

"That Annija had a child she was hiding ..." He paused, raised his head, and pinned Adam with a stare. "You're a father. You must understand what that did to me. She had a secret life she didn't care to share with me." Emil's gaze fell to his lap.

"Emil, Ludis was searching for something. After the flames died, he reached into the backseat and yanked out a video camera. He just tossed it away. What was he looking for?"

Emil's eyes widened, then his body seemed to crumple in on itself. His breaths came in quick, shaky gasps.

"What's wrong? Should I call Reese?"

Emil took in a deep breath, then another. Air was going in but no air was coming back out. His body was being starved of oxygen and he was suffocating. There was only one person who could help his grandfather stop hyperventilating. "Robert, I need your help."

Robert knelt next to Emil, lifting his wrist. When Robert entered the room, he had been a soldier. In seconds, he somehow converted back to a full-blown clergy.

"Mr. Vasnev. Try to take in a deep breath for me," Robert's voice was low and soothing.

It took several tries, but Robert finally calmed Emil's breathing. As soon as Emil could speak, his words twisted in Adam's gut.

"I thought he was after you because of my will. If you didn't appear before I died, most of my wealth and all my power would have been converted to you, with a substantial trust fund for Anna. Ludis could have fought the will and won because there is no proof you existed." He eyed Adam with a slight smile gracing the corners of his mouth. "When you disappear, you do a fine job."

"If that's not it, then why is he after me?"

Emil gripped on Adam's wrist, his bony fingers digging into the skin. "My brilliant daughter made sure you held the key to surviving by leaving you the only proof that can send Ludis to hell. And from the look on your face, you don't even know the power you hold over him."

Chapter Thirteen

Emil's words rang inside Adam's head. What shocked him to the core was the look of satisfaction that shone in his grandfather's eyes. Adam's gaze sought out Calista, who sat in a lounge chair, Anna fast asleep in her arms. Their eyes held for an instant before she lowered hers and brushed a strand of hair off Anna's cheek. The simple loving gesture slammed deep into his gut. He ached for moments like this in his life. Instead, he stood alone. He was so damn tired of being alone.

Robert, looking nothing like the priest he was only moments ago, rose and edged closer to Calista.

Adam yanked his wrist free from Emil's vice grip. "I don't have a clue what you are talking about. My mother didn't leave me anything. If she had, I would have exposed Ludis years ago."

Emil shot off the sofa. "No, you must have it. Annija ran to you, not me. You must have the proof." He again grabbed Adam's arm with a shaky hand. "I should have killed the little bastard when I caught him trying to rape Annija when she was fourteen. She pleaded for his life. Had there been even a hint of his involvement in Annija's death, I would have ripped the little bastard's balls off and stuffed them down his throat."

"How in the hell did you not suspect that motherfucker?" Adam yanked his arm from his grandfather's grip. "Whatever the hell you think Annija had, she didn't give it to me."

Emil shoved Adam in the chest with such force, he stumbled backward into the coffee table. He would have fallen flat on his ass if Robert hadn't caught him. Emil jerked open the small door of the end table and retrieved a compact semi-automatic pistol. Robert eyed the weapon before Adam and started to reach for it, but Emil had it rammed into Robert's chest an instant later. "Bullshit. Tell me what you know or ..."

Adam clinched hold of his Glock like it was an extension of his hand. "Put it down, Emil. He's a priest for God's sake."

"I'm going to hell anyway. But not before I make Ludis pay. Now tell me what I need to know."

Adam steadied his stance. The dying old man had morphed into the vicious crime boss right before his eyes. And to think he imagined for an instant that Emil could have changed.

"Reese, guards!" Emil's voice was strong, hard, and the frail persona of only a minute ago became an illusion.

Again men seemed to come out of the walls. The room filled, each man holding a gun on Adam. Robert inched a couple steps to his left so that he and Adam blocked Calista and Anna. There was no way Robert could protect them from the guards or Reese who stood directly behind them.

"What the hell, Emil. I can't give what I don't have."

"No, you must. Annija went to you. You have it. I know you have it!"

"What the fuck am I supposed to have?"

"The disk ... the disk from the camera in the car."

A light went off in Adam's head. The video camera Ludis tossed back into his mother's charred car had haunted his dreams. Taking a slow step forward, Adam caught his grandfather's wild, unfocused gaze. "I want Ludis as badly as you do. He took Rina from me. We just need to work together ... "

"No! You're lying to me."

Emil twisted away from Robert and jabbed the pistol into Adam's cheek. A rough edge cut into the skin, drawing blood. Adam froze, his breath caught in his throat.

"Emil, stop," Reese demanded from behind him, his voice low, controlled.

"He's lying. Ludis is lying again."

The pistol barrel shook against Adam's cheek while Emil's eyes darted back and forth in their socket, the wild look a mixture of intense hatred and pain. The man was on the edge—one false move, and he would turn bat-ass crazy.

Adam could end this by pulling the trigger. Emil would drop like a rock. But then what? How would he ever get over killing his own grandfather? Emil, driven mad from grief and the pain from a cancer eating him alive, had no idea what he was doing.

Adam quickly glanced at Calista. Miraculously, Anna still slept in her arms. Calming his breathing, he deliberately lowered the tone of his voice and said, "Reese, trust me."

Not waiting for a reply, Adam slapped his right hand hard against his grandfather's wrist while he grabbed the barrel of the gun with the other. He pushed the barrel down and away from him at the exact moment the fingers of his right hand gripped the bottom meat of Emil's thumb, forcing Emil to loosen his grip on the weapon. The move took only seconds. Emil let out a roar, but Adam retrieved the pistol and tossed it across the room. Emil came back with a hard jab to Adam's jaw, which Adam dodged. He took a fistful of Emil's collar, twisted him until his back was against Adam's front, and wrapped his arm tightly against his grandfather's neck. Leaning his head close to Emil's ear, he said, "Stop. I'm not Ludis." Adam's eyes darted to Calista. "Get my daughter out of here."

Calista came out of the chair. Anna jerked awake and squirmed out of her arms. It was a move Adam and she had played often. Wide-eyed, Anna took a step toward him. "Anna, stop. Go back to Calista. Reese, tell your men to lower their weapons. My daughter …"

"Do it!" Reese replied at the same time Emil screamed, "No! Shoot him, shoot him."

Adam tightened his hold. "I'm not Ludis. It's Adam."

Calista placed her hand on Anna's shoulder and tried to move her through the doorway, but Anna jerked free and ran across the room. Adam's heart dropped to his stomach. She was inches from Emil. "Stop," he said, the words coming out in a breathless hiss.

Emil faced Anna with a wide-eyed, frantic glare. "Annija, come to me, now." He reached out for her, but Adam tightened his hold.

"Stop. That's my daughter, Anna."

"Annija, listen to Papa. Come to me."

"I swear I'll snap your neck in two if you touch her."

Anna took another step but froze without speaking to Adam. He didn't know what he would have done if another blind-plowing pain sliced through his head at that moment. Instead, her entire concentration was on Emil. The next instant, she closed the distance between them and wrapped her arms around Emil's knees.

Adam saw red. He sucked in a shaky breath and shot a glare at Reese. "I won't let him ..."

Reese didn't say a word but jerked his head in a nod.

Emil glanced down at Anna and the tension in him drained. His shoulders slumped as he brushed his free hand over the back of her hair. He then reached into his suit pocket and removed his handkerchief, swiping it over his face. Never taking his eyes off Anna, he said, "You can release me."

"Who the hell am I?"

"Adam, my grandson."

Adam released his hold, and with his free hand, lifted Anna in his arms, handing her over to Robert. He then eased Emil down to the sofa.

Adam had always thought of himself as a clear thinker. This time, he couldn't connect the dots. Emil's eyes cleared and the man he met only a few minutes earlier returned. "What the hell just happened?" he asked Reese.

"It's the drug. It takes care of the pain, but there are side effects. He doesn't usually turn so ... "

"Fucking violent?"

Calista let out a sharp hiss. "Adam."

Again, he sucked in a cleansing breath and tried to calm his racing heart. His grandfather's tear-filled eyes were still on Anna. "I'm sorry. I don't think I would have hurt you," the old man mumbled.

"If I had anything from Annija, I would have told you."

"Annija went to her grave believing I ... she must have thought I planned the whole thing, sacrificed her to my enemy." His eyes bore into Adam. "She never knew how much I loved her, cherished her. I could have never been part of that butchery." Lowering his head, his shoulders shook as he wept.

All these years, Adam believed his mother had raced back into his life because Emil had found out about him. There was something else much more serious going on. Why had his mother come to him? At eighteen, how could he have possibly protected her?

"That day, my mother sent me away with only the clothes on my back and a small backpack. There wasn't anything but cash and a set of keys for a car she hid for me." Adam raised his hand when Reese started to speak. "And no, the car was completely clean. I went over every cranny. If there was any kind of disk, I sure as hell don't have it."

"You must! If not, my daughter's death was for nothing."

"Don't you get it, old man? My mother's death *was* for nothing."

Never had Adam wanted to strike someone more than at that moment. A hand pressed his elbow. He didn't have to turn to know it was Calista. "I wasn't going to ..."

"I know. I'm not here for him." She eased closer to him, placing her other hand around his waist. With her mouth close to his ear, she whispered, "I'm here for you." She then rested her head against his back. The tension in his shoulders and back muscles drained out of him. An instant later, another piercing pain sliced through his head followed by Anna's panicked voice.

"He's here. The man that hurt Mommy is here."

Chapter Fourteen

Adam's entire body stiffened instantly and his eyes grew glassy. He raised his hand and pressed his fingers to his temples.

Calista rubbed his back. Sweat broke out on his forehead and a groan escaped from his throat. "Exhale, Adam, and breathe through it."

He shot her a bone-chilling stare, then searched the room. What the hell was going on now?

"What did Anna say?"

"Ludis is here."

Every curse word in Calista's vocabulary screamed through her head. Father Anthony met her in the middle of the room and set Anna down between them. The move had only one meaning. Father Anthony wanted his hands free. Calista leaned the child against her body. She wanted to be closer to Adam, but his friend blocked him from her.

Adam drew his weapon, holding it at his side, and eased closer to his grandfather. He might not be ready to accept Emil with open arms, but his instinct to protect was crystal clear.

Emil tried to rise, but Adam placed a hand on his shoulder. "How does Anna know Ludis is here?" the old man asked.

A shadow appeared in the doorway and Ludis Vasnev stepped into the room.

"Yes, Blake, do tell us how your daughter knows what she shouldn't."

Calista's heart dropped to her stomach. The man she saw running from Anna's home stood only a few feet from Adam. It took everything in her to not race across the space to protect him. When did she become so brave? Pitted against a man like Ludis, she didn't hold a chance in hell of being successful. And the last thing she needed to do was bring attention to herself, making herself another target Adam had to protect.

Waves of fury radiated off Ludis and Adam, and they sliced through Calista, turning her cold to the bone. She had never experienced such hatred before. She drew Anna closer to her and took her hand in hers. Together, they tried to back into a corner. One of Ludis's men at the doorway lifted his semi-automatic rifle in his hand. Calista, rooted in place, hugged Anna tightly against her and focused on the weapon strapped across his chest.

Adam raised his gun, breaking the trance-like state in the room. "You just made my life so much easier, Uncle." Never taking his eyes off Ludis, he murmured, "Robert, get Anna and Calista out of here."

Before Father Anthony had a chance to react, two men with burr haircuts, neck tattoos, and tight lips that hadn't smiled in years appeared in the doorway, blocking the exit. At the same time, two more armed men charged in from the only other door in the room.

"I don't think so, Blake," Ludis sneered and shot Calista a stare. "No one is going anywhere. Why don't you introduce me to your friend?"

Ludis moved into Calista's personal space. A shiver crept up her spine as his eyes raked the length of her. If there was a way she could shower off that look, she would scour her skin until it turned red.

"She is the nanny and has nothing to do with us."

Adam's tone was harsh, unfeeling. Calista didn't dare glance in his direction. His earlier words, *get out anyway you can,* raced through her head. He was counting on her to protect Anna, but she had no idea how she was going to make it past Ludis's thugs.

Ludis reached out to place his hand on Anna's head. Before Calista could pull her away, Anna knocked his arm. This time, she didn't hide her face into Calista's side but glared at her great uncle with unbridled contempt.

"So, you know who I am, little one," he said, and knelt down until he was eye to eye with Anna.

Calista stared at what she could only describe as true evil. An image of Rina's lifeless body flashed in front of her and she couldn't control the shudder. She swallowed the fear and squared her shoulders. Maybe she couldn't fight like Adam, but the only way Ludis Vasnev was getting to Anna was through her.

He grabbed Anna's arm and tried to pull her away from Calista.

"Don't. Touch. Her." Adam took an angry step forward and cocked his weapon.

Emil shot up from the sofa. "Lay one hand on the child and I'll rip it off and shove it down your throat."

Ludis let out a harsh laugh. "So much love for your only son, old man. I'm touched." With the slightest movement of his hand as he rose, his men moved in and surrounded them.

Ludis reached for the medicine bottle on the coffee table and gave it a quick glance. "Is this how you are managing the pain from the cancer eating you from inside out?" He opened the bottle and emptied the pills into the palm of his hand. "You told me after I broke my arm at ten that pain meds were a sign of weakness. Weak men don't rule." He allowed the pills to spill to the floor. He then used the heel of his boot to ground them into a white powder. "I don't take orders from you."

Adam's grandfather's eyes darkened. He rose and charged toward his son. He raised his hand and backhanded Ludis, knocking him off balance.

"I have no son, you fucking bastard. You're dead, you hear me, dead!"

With each word, Emil's posture weakened and he struggled to stand. It was as if that one slap drained every ounce of his life energy. He sucked in a raspy breath and began to cough. Reaching for several tissues on the end table, he wiped his mouth. The thin, white paper came back dark red.

Ludis touched his lip and wiped away a small drop of blood, then lifted his hand and backhanded his father. Emil crumpled to his knees.

Calista let out a gasp and pulled Anna's head into her side, but knew she was too late to prevent Anna from seeing the violence.

"Enough!" Adam's body shook with such fury; his control was in threads.

Calista never saw Ludis move. One second he was glaring at his father and the next, he whipped around, drew his hand gun, and pointed it right at Anna. "I don't think so, Blake. Back down, now. Your bastard means next to nothing to me."

"No!" Emil let out in a raspy voice then began to cough again.

Father Anthony wheeled on Ludis, jerking his gunned hand into the air. The gun went off, shattering the stillness as the roar of the weapon ricocheted off the walls. The bullet hit the ceiling fixture and tiny shards of glass rained down on Ludis and Adam.

The two men behind the sofa rushed Adam. He pivoted and shot one of them in the right leg while flipping his weapon out of his hands into the air. His foot landed squarely in the man's lower groin area. He dodged the other man's swing, sending a lightning blow into the guy's nose, bone to bone. The man lost his footing, leaving him wide open for a hard gut punch.

Calista's mind ran in slow motion, detached from the scene until she felt Anna jerk. One minute the child was leaning against her with her head buried into Calista's side, and the next, she dashed around the man guarding the hallway. Another blast from Ludis's weapon sent shockwaves through Calista, rattling her bones. The white fabric of Emil's shirt began to turn red. His eyes widened in horror and he clutched his abdomen just below his rib cage.

God, Anna!

Calista turned back toward the exit. With her heart pounding violently against her chest, she slammed her shoulder into the man as they reached the doorway simultaneously. She wasn't strong enough to knock him down, but he did lose his footing and stagger back. That slight hit gave Calista the advantage she needed to race after Anna.

Calista sprinted past the stairway. A second and maybe a third gun went off behind her until the sitting room began to sound like a shooting range. She gasped for air and peered down the wing directly in front of the stairs. Anna wasn't there. Pivoting, she raced down the hallway to the entrance of the third wing. A quick glance over her shoulder gave her some relief. The hallway remained deserted. The guard hadn't followed her.

She caught sight of Anna just as she entered the third room on the right. A loud crash sounded from Emil's sitting room followed by more rapid gunfire. Calista clamped her lips tightly together to keep from screaming out. She darted through the doorframe behind Anna.

The room may have been elegant once, but now it housed an odd collection of deserted furniture. A long bar took up most of the back wall. She spotted Anna immediately as the child struggled to open two cabinet doors under the bar.

"Anna, come. We can't stay in here. We'll be trapped if anyone comes through the door," Calista said. She reached for Anna's hand, but the little girl jerked free and shook her head. Anna continued to yank on the knob of the left door, but it didn't budge.

"What are you doing?" Calista bent and glanced under the bar.

Anna's lips moved and a rasping sound came from her throat. She slammed a frustrating palm against the door and peered at Calista. Her eyes filled with tears and a soft sound escaped her lips.

"My God, Anna. Try again. Talk to me."

"Help me, please," Anna said.

Calista dropped down on her knees. "Oh my, you have the sweetest voice. Do you want the cabinet opened?"

Anna nodded.

Glancing at the door, Calista said, "I don't know why you want to get in here so badly, but it must be important. Move over and let me at it."

A slight smile appeared on the child's face. As Calista took both cabinet knobs in her hands and gave a hard jerk. The doors swung open, almost knocking Calista on her butt. The doors hid a very narrow staircase that disappeared into blackness.

"You don't think you're going down there, do you?" she said, swallowing hard. "No way in hell are we going down there."

"It's safe."

Calista could only gape at the four-year-old. "How do you know? How did you even know this was here?"

Anna swallowed and tried to speak. The sound appeared to be stuck in her throat.

"Try again."

"She said this was the way out."

"Who is she?"

"Annija."

This time it was Calista's eyes that filled. "Dear God, how is this happening?"

She pulled Anna into her arms and held her. If Adam's mother was helping her granddaughter, who in the hell was she to argue.

"Does Annija know where there is a flashlight?"

Anna let out a giggle and shook her head. The wooden stairwell was very dark, like hellish dark. At best, the steps led to some kind of cellar. Great, she could use a good, stiff drink.

Glancing at Anna's trusting expression, Calista shoved her fear down deep and said, "Okay, you win. I'll go first, but I want you to hold on to my belt loop very tightly. Can you do that?"

"Yes," Anna nodded, a smile beaming on her face.

Her voice sounded so wonderful to Calista's ears, she couldn't help smiling. She opened the cabinets wide and took one step, then another. Placing both hands against the walls on either side of the stairway, she rocked gently back and forth, but the stairs remained steady. At least she and Anna wouldn't fall to their deaths into the dark pit.

Anna's small hands clutched onto Calista's belt.

"We'll take two more steps, but then we have to close the cabinet doors. It's going to be much darker." She turned and glanced at Anna. "Are you okay with that?"

Anna swallowed and peered into the darkness. It took her a moment, but she nodded.

Calista took the steps slowly then reached over Anna's head to pull the cabinet doors shut. The small knob came off in her hands. She tried to grab the edge of the wood but she couldn't get the door to latch. Angry voices sounded in the wing, sending a chill down her spine. There was no time to take care of details.

"Shit! Hang on, Anna. Just stay very close to me," she whispered, and began to quickly work their way to the bottom. The stairwell opened into a room, but the light from above only gave a hint of its features. The only thing Calista could tell was the walls were carved from stone and had a circular slant.

Anna had a death grip on her belt. Calista reached back and placed a hand on her shoulder. She wasn't feeling a bit brave, but the child needed her to be. She took one step into the cellar and paused.

"Crap. I forgot all about my phone." Calista dug into her pocket.

Fear had her so tense, she forgot all about the flashlight app. She raised the phone above her head and pressed a button. The chamber filled with a hint of blue light. It wasn't much, but she could at least see where she was going.

Across the chamber, two tunnels came out of the back wall. Calista glanced down at Anna. "Which way?"

The child shrugged, tilted her head to the side, and studied the two tunnels. She lifted her hand and pointed to the one closest to them.

Calista took three steps into the dark tunnel then staggered backward. The invisible webbing that extended the length of the opening now covered her from head to toe.

"Shit, shit, shit," she yelped as she brushed the sticky threads from her hair, face, and body. She wiped a hand down her bare arms. If the web was that huge, where the hell was the spider? "I hate spiders, damn it," she hissed. "Now I'm going to feel those creepy-crawly little monsters all over me."

Anna let out a giggle. The innocent sound, even in her spider-hating moment, eased the tension from Calista's shoulders.

With the cell phone light on, she could only see a couple of feet in front of her. The passage narrowed slightly and the chill in the musky air gave her goose bumps. She kept her fingertips on the wall despite her repulsion of what she might find there.

The short tunnel led into another room that wasn't quite as dark as the first chamber. Rows of old wine racks filled the space. A few still contained bottles of forgotten wine covered completely in dust and spider webs. The air was thick and chilled Calista to the bone. Anna let out a loud sneeze. Moving into the room, Calista glanced back at Anna still holding onto her belt loop.

"Where to?"

Anna tried to speak, but when the words wouldn't come, she pointed to a door at the opposite end of the room. Calista began to cross the room. An instant later, Anna froze, pulling on Calista's waist.

"What's wrong, Anna?"

She pointed to her foot.

Calista stared down at the floor. "Where is your shoe?"

Anna shrugged, glancing back at the tunnel.

Shining the cell phone light back the way they'd came, she could just see the tip of a sneaker peeking out in the dark. "Wait right here. I'm going back into the tunnel for your shoe."

Anna seemed okay until Calista entered the tunnel. She let out a loud gasp and choked out, "He's coming!"

A double dose of fear shot through Calista. She scooted a couple more inches into the tunnel, grabbed the shoe, and hurried back to Anna. She lifted her in her arms and dashed across the room to the door.

"No, hide," Anna said as she struggled out of Calista's arms.

Calista reached for Anna's hand and edged down the side of the wall. She shut off her phone but kept her fingers clenched around the base in the now darkened room. At the back wall, they eased around a stack of discarded, broken wine crates. The last rack in the row sat at a slight angle, leaving just enough room for Calista to ease Anna into a space against the cool, stone wall then crouch down next to her.

Angry voices sounded close. Calista rose, but Anna grabbed her hand.

"I'll be right back, but I have to borrow your shoe."

Anna nodded and released her hand. Calista charged out of the row and heaved the shoe toward the large wooden door. It landed with a soft thump just as Calista settled down next to Anna. The scared child squirmed into her lap and hid her face into Calista.

Placing a hand over Anna's head, Calista drew her tightly against her chest as loud, heavy footsteps echoed from the tunnel. Someone was heading right toward them, and she had nothing to protect Anna but her cell phone. Calista tried to slow her rapid breathing and whispered in Anna's ear. "Are you still talking to your dad?"

Anna shook her head no.

Calista couldn't see the men who entered the room, but Ludis's deep, gruff voice came out loud and pissed.

"Search every inch of the fucking place."

A moment later, a beam of light shot down the row. Anna stared at Calista. With her finger to her lips, Calista mouthed, "Don't move."

Staring through the tiny cracks in the backboard of the wine rack, Calista shuddered as a man holding a handgun in one hand and a high beam flashlight in the other paused in front of her. Fear gripped her heart and she reached out to her personal angel. *Hanna, please help me keep Anna safe.*

Anna soundlessly pressed her face into Calista's shoulder while Calista held her breath. Just as he moved to shine the light in their direction, one of Ludis's men shouted, "I found something."

The man eased away from the wall and headed back the way he came. Calista leaned her head against the cold stone. Anna shifted and glanced at her. She moved a strand of hair off of the girl's forehead before placing her finger to her mouth. The men were close, only a few feet away. Any sound would bring them back and there would be no place to run.

The noise from Ludis and his men lessened until there was only silence. Calista glanced down at Anna.

"Are they gone?"

The child closed her eyes and took in a breath. Time stilled as Calista waited. A hint of a smiled formed at the corner of Anna's lips and she opened her eyes.

"He's gone."

Calista set Anna down next to her and stood. She eased out from behind the rack and took one step into the row when the cellar door screeched open, spilling a dim light into the room. Slowly, she moved back behind the wine rack. Anna's breathing grew heavy, and even the arm she wrapped around the frightened child didn't seem to help.

They both froze as Ludis strolled into view. He took two steps past them and glanced along the back wall. His flashlight ran from the top to the bottom of the rack. He then turned and positioned his light over the racks on the opposite side of the row. He turned back toward them. Calista eased away from the hole and held her breath. She could feel Ludis's glare piercing through her, sending a chill up her spine. After what seemed like an eternity, he turned and made his way out of the row.

"I know you are in here. Tell Blake all I want is the disk. I will leave you alone if he just hands it over." She heard the door scrape open and close.

Calista's lungs burned. She exhaled. Rooted to her spot, she glanced down at Anna and their gazes held. "Your dad? Is he okay?"

"I don't know."

The horrific image of Emil's bloodstained shirt flickered in her head as the memory of the rapid gunfire roared between her ears. Adam couldn't be hurt, bleeding. She may still be fuming that he investigated every crumb of her life, but damn it, the stubborn, pigheaded man had to be alright. Calista refused to believe anything else.

"Let's get out of here."

Calista moved out of the hiding place and reached her hand down to Anna. Just as they moved from behind the rack, pounding footsteps sounded from the tunnel.

"Shit," Calista whispered and shoved Anna back again between the rack and the wall. Neither made a sound as their eyes bore into each other. Several beams of light flashed down the row and bounced off the back wall. Heavy footsteps headed right toward them. The light showed right into the hole, making Calista squint. A hand clamped down around Calista's elbow and yanked her out from behind the rack. Her chest slammed into a man's muscular chest, hard.

"Don't you ever scare me like that again," Adam's deep voice cracked.

Chapter Fifteen

"Anna, come out from behind there." Adam picked up Anna and gave her a fierce hug. Setting her back down, he kept his arm around his daughter as he wrapped his other hand around Calista's waist, lifting her up so they were eye to eye. "God, Calista ... "

The rest of his words stuck in his throat. He didn't know how to convey his fear nor the overwhelming gratitude he felt for the woman in his arms, so he did the only thing that made sense. He brought his lips down on hers. The darkness kept him from reading her expression, but she wasn't struggling against him. Her arms circled his neck and she molded her body to his. It was as if she were holding on to him for dear life right before she deepened the kiss.

She broke away for an instant and said, "I heard the gunfire. I thought you ..."

Her breath hitched and she brought his mouth back to hers. The kiss was quick, hard, demanding. Adam could feel the moisture threatening to spill from the corner of his eyes. "I watched you shoulder-slam one of Ludis's men and go after Anna." As he held her against him with one arm, he brought the other up and cupped her face. "You tackled a man with a semi-automatic. Shit. I almost pissed my pants."

Adam curled a hand around the nape of her neck and lowered his mouth back to hers. It was meant to be just a kiss, but the moment their lips joined, something wild and feral coursed through his veins, making him forget for an instant all that surrounded him. He owed her *everything*.

Adam never felt so damn helpless in his life, not even when Rina lay dying on the floor. At least he'd had the chance to kill her attackers. The moment Ludis broke free of Robert's hold and went after Anna and Calista, something dark broke from deep inside Adam. He tore through Ludis's men like they were paper dolls and dodged the bullets flying about the room.

Anna wrapped her arms around his knee. He broke the kiss, but keeping his left arm around Calista, he picked up Anna with his right arm. He couldn't prevent the tremor that sliced through him as he held them both to him.

"How did you know where to find us?" Calista's voice was rough and husky.

"Anna told me."

Robert joined them. "Are you two okay?"

"We're fine. Ludis and his men left through there," Calista said, pointing to the old wooden door across the room.

"I don't give a fuc…"

Robert placed a hand on his shoulder then reached for Anna. "Come with me for a moment, sweetheart. Your dad needs a moment alone with Calista."

Adam kissed his daughter's cheek then handed her over to his friend. "Give me five," he said, barely able to form words. "Don't go upstairs without me."

"We'll be in the first chamber. Take your time."

Robert wrapped his coat around Anna and headed down the row. Adam didn't wait to pull Calista back into his arms. They clung to each other, both breathing hard.

Several moments passed before Calista broke the silence. "We were both fine."

"I'm so damn sorry, Calista. I never wanted you involved in any of this."

She covered his lips with her fingers. "Don't. Stop blaming yourself for things that are completely out of your control. Ludis left a message for you."

"He found you and let you go?"

"He stood right here." Calista shuttered and pointed to the spot on the floor. "After what seemed like a lifetime, he turned and glared right at me through the crack in the wood, spoke, then just walked away."

"And his message?"

"If you hand over the disk, he will leave us all alone. It's all he wants."

The last words were muffled. Calista had buried her head into his chest. Adam drew her hard against him as her soft sobs wracked her body.

"I got you. It's over. I promise it's over for you."

Adam drew Calista into an embrace. For the first time in a long time, he held a woman in his arms and didn't immediately start calculating how he was going to walk away. There was so much depth underneath that sweet, girl-next-door persona she proudly wore that he ached for just one chance to get to know the real Calista Martin.

Calista raised her head and swiped a hand over her moist cheek. "No, it's not over, Adam. Your uncle will never stop until he has what he wants and you will never give in to him."

She knew him that well at least. He had no idea what was on the disk, but if he ever got his hands on it, he sure the hell wouldn't hand it over to Ludis.

"What are you going to do?"

One way or another, he was getting Calista and Anna out of his nightmare. He stepped back, the better to grab her full attention. "I have to find the disk and then take care of Ludis."

"By yourself?"

"No, not this time. You were right. I need help. Jared and Noah will back me up. And Calista, I'll come back for you and Anna. You have to believe that."

She appeared torn for a moment, one eyebrow raised and her forehead wrinkled, as if judging whether he was sincere or merely trying to hoodwink her into staying out of the way again.

"There is something you need to know before you leave."

"What?"

"Anna is talking to your mother."

He didn't think it was possible, but those six words jolted his heart. "What?"

"I knew about this place because Anna led me here." Calista eased around him and moved down the row to the center of the cellar. "Anna is speaking to me. Not long sentences, but a few words." She pointed to the row they just left. "She was the one who told me where to hide from Ludis. When I asked her how she knew about the secret passage in the bar, she told me her *Annija* told her."

Adam ran both hands through his hair and rubbed the back of his neck. "That's ..."

"Impossible?" Calista raised her arms. "Look around you. How would I have ever have found this place? What you have here, Adam, is a miracle." Her voice grew soft, quiet, but it echoed against the stone walls. "You are not alone in any of this. I don't think you have ever been alone. Your mother is trying to help you and Anna is your connection to her."

The acid that lived in the pit of his stomach churned into his throat. It burned like hell, but he welcomed the pain. It made sense. The last several hours had yanked Adam completely out of what he understood about the world and into something he wasn't ready to accept.

Yet Calista didn't seem to have any trouble believing the impossible. How could she accept what was happening to them so easily?

He took a step backward. "No, damn it. This doesn't make any sense. My mother is dead. Period! There has to be another explanation. I'm not playing this game nor am I involving my little girl in this nightmare another minute."

Adam's heart shuttered. He couldn't catch his breath. He reached for Calista, needing her near him. "You are out too,

Calista." He ran his hands up and down her arms before pulling her into him. "I'm finding a safe place for both of you. No argument, no discussion."

"I think we are way past doing what you want to do, Adam Blake. If you don't listen to what Anna has to say, you may just destroy any chance you have of a real life with your daughter."

"You expect me to … "

"Not me. Annija, your mother." Calista fisted her hands on his chest.

Adam shut his eyes and allowed a tear to slip over his eyelid and down his cheek. He was a seasoned soldier who had seen more heartache and destruction to last him multiple lifetimes. None of it touched what he was feeling at that moment in the darkness of a forgotten cellar.

Anna and Annija.

If he allowed himself to accept the possibility his mother was still there for him … the very thought contradicted everything he ever allowed himself to believe.

Without weighing his decision, he reached out for Calista again. He needed something real, solid in his arms to center him. He could feel the rapid beat of her heart through her T-shirt.

"Calista, I don't know what to do. This is so far out of my understanding."

Her lips covered his in a soft, sensual kiss that almost brought him to his knees. As quickly as it began, she broke away, and stepped out of his hold. This time she took his face in her hands.

"You have been in fight mode since Anna's first contact. Ludis may have left, but he's not done with any of us. As you said, your brothers have your back." She teased the hair at the back of his neck. "I don't know how to deal with all of this anymore than you do. I *do* know you want to go after Ludis but Anna needs you more." Calista traced her finger down the side of his jaw. "Pete always told me that things kind of fall into place after a good sleep. You are no good to anyone until you rest. Can we just get out of here and then decide what comes next?"

Robert barged back into the cellar holding Anna.

"We have to go. One of your grandfather's men said Emil is in real bad shape."

Adam took Calista's hand and raced out of the cellar into the tunnel. Once back upstairs, he drew his gun and kept Calista behind him.

"Robert, can you keep Anna away?"

"You deal with Emil and I'll take care of Anna."

Remembering the condition of the room he left just minutes before, he paused before saying to Calista, "You should stay here with Robert."

"No, I'm with you."

A deep sadness edged into her eyes. Dread hit him hard. Instead of wasting time convincing her to stay back, he reached for her hand and headed toward the sitting room. At the doorway, he eased her behind him and entered.

Emil sat on the floor with his back against the sofa. Reese held pressure on a wound inches below Emil's heart. As soon as Emil noticed Adam, he gasped out, "Ludis?"

Adam knelt down and placed two fingers on his grandfather's neck. He waited for a pulse to bounce back against his skin. It was slow and unsteady. He met Reese's stare.

"Stomach wound. I can't stop the bleeding. His blood is thinned from the steroids he is taking. I called 911."

Adam rose and searched the room for the portable oxygen tank he noticed earlier. He set it down next to Emil and placed the mask over his grandfather's face before delivering the bad news. "Ludis got away. I'll worry about him. You need to relax and just breathe."

Emil closed his eyes and tried to do just that. Adam could tell he was in pain. Perhaps there were enough pieces of the pills that Ludis hadn't ground to provide some relief. He crawled over to that spot in the carpet and dug out several of the larger chunks. Reaching for the water on the end table, he brought it to his grandfather's mouth. "Here, take this. It will ease some of the pain."

Emil swallowed only a small sip, but it was enough to get the medicine down his throat. Then he grabbed Adam's hand in a weak squeeze.

"Adam, I wanted more time. So sorry ... "

The words rippled through Adam's heart. When in the hell did he start caring about a man he hated as much as Emil Vasnev?

Reese cleared his throat. "You need to get out of here. You can't be here when the police arrive. Too many questions you don't want to answer."

Adam clung to his grandfather's hand. Each pulse grew weaker than the one before. "No, I'm staying."

"Think of Anna. You need to get her someplace safe, then take care of Ludis."

Grief lodged in Adam's throat. He didn't know what to do. He sought out Calista. Tears filled her eyes as she stared back at him.

"You keep him alive, damn it. Understand?" He practically growled at Reese.

"He's dying, Adam. You're a soldier. You know what a wound like this can do."

He could only nod. In the distance, he could hear the sirens moving toward them.

Reese clamped his other hand on Adam's shoulder. "Take the car. My driver will get you back to the small airport. Ludis will be seeking the disk. You need to get to it before him."

"Why? What the hell is on that disk?"

"I have no idea. Whatever it is, Ludis wants it bad enough to go against Emil."

"Adam," Emil said in a pain-filled whisper.

Adam lowered his head to his grandfather's lips.

"My Annija made a fine … man." He pressed Adam's hand and his eyes floated to the back of his eyelid. The lids closed and he gasped out a groan.

As the sirens grew closer, Emil Vasnev's head tilted to the side and he took his last breath.

Adam leaned in and placed his lips on Emil's forehead. He tried to express some kind of prayer, but his mind froze. A hand rested on his shoulder and Adam met his best friend's gaze. The priest was back and Adam had never been so happy to see him.

"I don't know how to … what to say … what to ask for."

"I do."

Robert removed a small canister from the inside of his pocket and placed a thin stole around his neck. Calista, holding Anna in her arms, knelt down next to Adam and took his hand in hers. Tears spilled onto Adam's cheeks and he let them fall. He cradled his daughter and Calista in his arms.

Robert dipped his hand into the blessed oil and placed the sign of the cross on Emil's forehead. He bowed his head and said a prayer of forgiveness. When he was done, he rose. Adam and Calista did the same. "We should go. He's in God's hands now."

Adam took Calista's hand in his and headed toward the door. He paused and glanced back at the man he hated for sixteen years.

"It's okay. Go," Reese said. "All Emil wanted since the day he found out about you was your safety and well being. He worked hard and planned well for that."

Again, Adam could only nod while Calista tugged on his hand. He turned toward the door and they raced down the stairway to the foyer. Moments later, they were in the car, driving away. On the road to the airport, several ambulances and police cars passed them.

They were in the air within five minutes of arriving at the airport. Calista sat next to him while Anna and Robert faced him.

No one spoke until Robert broke the silence. "What's the plan?"

Adam began to speak but Calista interrupted. "Adam is going to sleep until we land." In response, he settled his head on her shoulder. There was no way he had the energy to argue with the determination etched in her every feature. Just as he closed his eyes, he said, "Robert, you know that prayer thing you do?"

"Yes."

"Can you ask ... I want Emil at peace so he can be with Annija."

Chapter Sixteen

Shut down, sleep, stop thinking about it.

Calista shot a quick glance at Adam in the seat next to her. His head rested against her shoulder, his spicy musk scent mingled in the air, surrounding her. He held her hand but was fast asleep. In fact, he hadn't stirred since the plane took off down the runway.

Never had she wanted to pinch herself more than now for acting like such a silly moron. It was just a kiss. If she were being truly honest with herself, it wasn't just one kiss. Adam had kissed her in that chilly, dusty cellar three times, like she really meant something to him. And it wasn't one of those "I was worried about you" brotherly kisses. No. Each one could only be classified as a mind-blowing, leg-shaking kiss that still vibrated through her system hours later.

Adam Blake could set her on edge from across the room. Up close and personal, he was lethal. The jerk may have just ruined all men for her ... for life.

There was such unleashed emotion in him that he sealed behind a thick wall. How many people in his life recognized the man behind the harsh exterior? Father Anthony? His brothers?

Calista used to watch people walk out of their way to keep clear of Adam in the diner. That used to break her heart even before she got to know the man he was with Anna. What a lonely isolated life he forced himself to live.

The diner, Pete—it all seem so distant. The last twenty-four hours had been such a turbulent rollercoaster ride that Calista couldn't keep it all straight in her head. What she did know was that she adored Anna and her father was growing on her like a kudzu vine. Pressing her other hand over his, she couldn't help murmuring, "Love it, hate it, it still grows on you."

"Did you say something, Calista?" Father Anthony asked quietly from the seat across her.

She could feel the heat rising up her neck and into her cheeks. "Just talking to myself."

"Can't sleep?"

"It's been a tough few hours. Hard to shut down."

The priest studied her for what seemed like a lifetime before he spoke. "He's worth it, you know."

"Excuse me?"

"Adam, he's a good man. Hard life but a good man underneath it all."

Calista glanced at Adam. "I know."

A grin spread across the priest's face. "What gave it away?"

She couldn't help but peek at Anna, who sat curled up against Father Anthony. The girl also fell into a deep sleep as soon as the plane was in the air. How did a four-year-old latch onto Calista's heart in such a short time?

"No man can love and care as deeply as Adam and not be a good man."

"That is a very astute observation." He paused again as if he was collecting his thoughts. "I would like to ask something of you."

Calista swallowed. "What?"

The man's features grew serious. "Don't let Adam shut you out of his life. He's going to need someone like you."

Her heart drummed between her ears, blocking out all sound for an instant. "Adam's life ... we don't really ..."

"I know he scares you, Calista, and that fear is justified. You have been through hell yourself since Hanna's death. That kind of violence leaves deep scars. What I'm suggesting is you give him a chance."

"He's going to run so fast, so far ... "

"A chance is all I'm asking."

The moment this plane landed, Adam was going to dump her and go after Ludis. She no longer considered that a great sin. Someone had to stop him, and she didn't know anyone more capable than Adam. As much as she wanted him safe, no one would ever be able to hold him back when his mind was made up. Adam was a protector.

Did Father Anthony understand what he was asking?

The woman who fell for Adam Blake wasn't getting a nine-to-five type of man. Pete always warned her that her life partner had to be a man she didn't want to change because she would never be able to change him. As she glanced at Adam from the corner of her eye, one thing stood out. Her heart might not survive it, but she wouldn't change a hair on that stubborn, obstinate, drop-dead gorgeous head.

"Father Anthony, I'll never give up on Adam, but I can't promise he will be around long enough to notice."

"He's already noticed, Calista."

The heat in her cheeks flared. To keep from having to figure out a reply, she took the chicken way out and closed her eyes. If she couldn't sleep before, she damn well wasn't falling asleep now.

• • •

The roar of the engines from the jet as it braked and taxied off the runway yanked Adam out of a dream-filled sleep. He shot up and gripped his armrest.

"Bad dream?" Calista asked from the seat next to him.

Bad dream didn't even come close to what the few minutes of shuteye put him through. His eyes scanned the inside of Emil's private plane. Robert sat with Anna curled up next to him fast asleep. Her stuffed elephant rested on her lap.

His heart hurt with how much he loved his little girl. She wasn't just a living example of the best this crap-shit world had to offer, but Anna kept him from crossing over so many lines. She made his life worth living.

What in the hell had he done for her but be the worst of fathers? He couldn't even call himself a father. Thomas McNeil was a father. Nothing came between him and his children. That was what Adam wanted for Anna.

But was he even capable of that kind of love and devotion? His world was consumed with violence. Could he shift gears, ridding his heart of revenge and live in Anna's world ... Calista's world? Emil gave him a front seat view of what his future would be like if he was incapable of change.

Images of the dream from his restless nap slipped back into his mind, making him stomp down on the shudder that yearned to slice through him. How he hated haunting dreams.

The first part of the dream was of Rina. She called out to him to keep their baby safe. He was trying.

The rest of the dream was almost too horrible to relive. Ludis had a gun rammed into Calista's right temple. He screamed at Adam, but everything he said was one massive fog. The next instant, Ludis fired his weapon and Calista dropped to the floor like a lifeless doll.

A shudder shocked Adam, clutching hold of his heart. Ludis needed to be stopped before he had a chance to re-group with whoever was working with him.

"Adam?" Calista touched his arm.

He met her gaze.

"What's the most important thing in your life?"

"It's not a what. It's who."

A smile graced her lips and she placed a hand on his cheek. "Then all is well. Pete says that things have a way of working out. There's no need to lose sleep over worrying."

Adam didn't know how to reply so he nodded. His life had never been that simple.

The plane came to a stop and the crew opened the door, lowering the stairs onto the asphalt. Adam rose and checked his weapon. He then reached down and cradled Anna into his arms. She woke, smiled at him, then rested her head on his shoulder.

Calista glanced out the small window. Her eyes widened as she said, "Where are we? I thought we were returning to Maryland."

"We can't go anywhere Ludis knows about."

"And this is?"

"It's a municipal airport west of Morgantown, West Virginia."

Adam pointed out the window. Two men leaned against the brick terminal. "Jared and Noah will take you to a cabin I own about fifty miles from here in the mountains. You and Anna will be safe there."

"You are coming with us, right?"

He shook his head.

"You told me you were going to allow your brothers to help you. You aren't going after Ludis alone."

"This is them helping me. I can take care of Ludis. What I need more than anything is to know that you and Anna are safe from him."

Color drained from her cheeks. "You don't even know where Ludis is."

"All I have to do is get the disk or make him believe I have his disk and he will find me." He reached for Calista's hand and brought it to his lips. "I keep my promises."

Calista turned to Robert. "You are going with him, aren't you?"

"Not this trip. Adam is better alone, Calista."

Adam positioned Anna's backpack on his shoulder and moved to the entrance of the plane. Once down the steps, Jared took Anna and gave her a hug. She clung to her uncle like they were old friends. It lightened Adam's heart knowing that Anna was comfortable with his brother.

Jared held out his hand and Adam took it in his. What he thought was just a handshake among friends turned into a hug—a brother hug.

Noah pulled him into his embrace and said, "You look like shit, bro."

"The last twenty-two hours haven't been much fun. Thanks for coming."

"That is what brothers do. We help each other out." Noah added.

Adam scrubbed a hand over his face. "I need … "

Jared placed his hand on Adam's shoulder. "I'll watch over Anna and Calista like a mother hen. You do what you need to do. We'll be here when you are done."

"We?"

"The rest of our siblings are on their way here."

"Shit. I guess they know."

"Yep. Jason wants to slug you," Jared grinned.

"Emma, too," Noah added. "But no worries there. She still hits like a girl no matter how many times I tried to teach her how to give a good jab.

"And Mac's good as long as you let him play with all your cool surveillance equipment at the cabin." Jared gave him a hard stare. "It's a long drive. I better get little sweet pea in her booster seat."

Adam kissed Anna's cheek, reveling in the scent of sleepy child. "I have to be away for a few days. Uncle Jared and Aunt Jennie are going to take very good care of you until I get back."

Anna squirmed out of her uncle's arms. Once her feet hit the ground, she dashed to Calista, pulling on her arm until she knelt. Anna cupped her hands over Calista's ear and whispered something.

Calista leaned back and stared. "Are you sure?"

Anna nodded.

"Is Anna speaking?" Jared asked him.

"Just to Calista. She hasn't said a word inside my head since we were at Emil's."

Anna wrapped Calista in a tight hug then strolled back to Jared. He took her hand and said, "We'll give you a moment alone with Calista." He turned and entered the terminal.

Adam studied her for several moments in awkward silence before he spoke. "I'll be back."

"I know."

He brushed a strand of hair away from her face then cupped her jaw. "And I'm hoping maybe we could go out for an evening, have a meal, maybe see a movie."

Calista let out a heavy sigh. "That would have been a better place to begin."

Adam leaned in and caressed her bottom lip with his, wishing he had the time to explore what being near her was doing to him. "I don't know what to say to you. Good-bye seems so final."

"How about I'll see you in a bit."

He chuckled and drew her against him. Part of him wanted to wrap his arms around her and take her with him, but his good sense took over. She was so much better off with his brothers. He curled his hand around the back of her neck and brought her lips back to his. One more taste to keep him going.

"See you in a bit, Calista." With a final wave, he entered the cabin of the jet.

He dropped into the same seat he exited only a few minutes ago. The steward took his jacket and stored it in the overhead bin.

"The pilot said we can take off anytime."

Adam didn't bother glancing up. "Now."

"Very well. Would you like a drink first?"

"Bourbon and leave the bottle."

The engines of the plane began to hum as the slick aircraft moved into position. A glass of amber liquor came into view. He reached for the short, round glass and froze.

"Hi, again," Calista said, holding the drink out to him.

"What the hell, Calista." Adam rose. "You are not going with me!"

She at least had the decency to blush before she shrugged and said, "Anna said I needed to be with you. So here I am."

"You can't allow a four-year-old to tell you what to do." Adam moved down the short hallway, tightened his hand into a fist, and banged on the door of the cockpit. He yanked it open and glared at the pilot. "Turn around. We're returning to the terminal." He then shot a look at Calista. "You are not coming with me. That's final."

"Annija said I needed to be with you. Are you seriously going to argue with your mother?"

The pilot interrupted. "Sir, what's it going to be? We have the okay."

Adam first glanced at the pilot then Calista. His heart roared between his ears. He wanted her there with him—he could admit that—but could he keep her safe?

Without taking time to second guess himself, he slammed the cockpit door shut and circled her waist with his arms. Lifting her body so she fit perfectly against his, he brought his lips back down on hers. A mixture of mind-blowing fear and sensual excitement roiled through him. Before Calista's overpowering essences took over, he broke away and charged back to his seat. Dropping down, he hooked his seatbelt in place and shot her a glare.

Calista eased down in the seat facing Adam. She buckled her seatbelt and folded her arms around her middle. "So, where are we going?"

"Home."

"Where is home?"

"California."

He scooted down in the seat and stretched out his legs in the seat next to Calista. He tilted his head to the side and closed his eyes. The last twenty-four hours had drilled home that he needed to ignore her when he was pissed; he didn't want to say something that he couldn't take back.

He didn't like being angry at Calista. Of course, if he were completely honest, he would admit he was angrier with himself. He should have been man enough to carry her petite, sexy as hell little body down the stairs, and dump her into the backseat of Jared's truck. She had no business in his nightmare.

The plane taxied back onto the runway. It took only minutes before the engines roared to life. Calista's hands clutched hold of the armrest for dear life as she gazed out the window.

"Calista."

She turned away from the window.

"Unlatch your seatbelt and get over here," he said, holding out his hand.

"I'm fine. I'll just have to get used to flying."

A low growl escaped his throat. "Look, if you are going to live through the next few hours, you need to follow my orders without question. If I tell you to sit, you sit. If I tell you to run, you damn well better run like hell, no looking back. No questions. Got it?"

"Yes, I got it."

"Then unlatch your damn seatbelt and get over here."

Surprisingly, she didn't argue. In seconds, she was sitting next to him, her grip almost cutting the circulation off in his left hand. He again leaned his head against the cushion headrest and allowed his tired eyes to ease closed as the plane took off.

A comfortable silence settled in the cabin. Calista rested her head on his shoulder. Unable to stop himself, he placed his arm around her and drew her tightly against him before he said, "If anything happens to you, I'll never forgive you ... or myself."

Chapter Seventeen

The arch-shaped French door stood wide open to the tile deck overlooking the Pacific Ocean. A light wind blew across the sand, perfuming the air with a salty aroma. Waves broke gently on the shore, sending up sprays of seawater over the rocks. Calista took in a deep breath and allowed the calm of the ocean to drain away the tension in her shoulders and lower back.

Adam stood motionless in the shadows off the patio, his gaze fixated on the horizon where the ocean met the black sky. Nothing about his stance was approachable.

She stepped back into the master bedroom. It was breathtaking with its vaulted, light-stained oak beam ceiling and a mixture of whitewash stain and painted walls. Soft blue and green accents added to the artfully arranged room. The only problem with the space was that it didn't represent Adam at all. The room was a showpiece, not a home.

Calista couldn't see Adam sleeping in the massive king-sized bed that sat in the middle of the room. The bed was staged, not a place that screamed out for the comfort of a good night sleep. In fact, this home held nothing—no photos, mementos—nothing of the man she was beginning to know.

Glancing out the window, she studied Adam. His silence was a thick, impenetrable wall. He closed himself off from her the moment he woke from a deep sleep on the plane. She could count on two hands the number of words they had shared since then.

After the plane landed in LAX, Adam pulled out a key from his pocket and opened the trunk of the only sedan parked in the lot for the private terminal. They drove in silence for more than an hour to a house that sat high in the hills overlooking the ocean.

Calista's heart hurt for the man who stood alone staring out into the night. From the moment Anna first screamed in his head, he wanted one thing: to keep the people in his world safe. Instead of respecting that, she had shoved herself right smack in the middle of it. Calista didn't doubt for a minute that Adam was more than capable of protecting her from Ludis. What frightened her to her toes was the length he would go to keep her safe.

Why in the hell did she get back on that damn plane? Had she completely lost her mind? Anna was a remarkable child, but she was just a child. Adam had every right to be angry.

Acting compulsively wasn't Calista's style, especially since Hanna's attack. She kept her world very small and safe. What she should have done was allow Adam to place her in a safe house from the very beginning. Instead, she'd thrown caution to the wind and held on tightly to a scared four-year-old.

On the other hand, there was only one way Anna could have known about the secret passage. Emil didn't tell her, so the only explanation was some freakin' crazy supernatural thing Calista couldn't see or understand. And then there was Anna's warning: *If you don't protect Daddy, I'll never see him again.*

If Calista dared tell Adam what Anna whispered in her ear right before the plane took off, he would lock her up and throw away the key. Adam was a highly trained fighter. Calista had never seen anyone move like him. She, on the other hand, hid behind her grandfather for the last year and a half, too frightened to even live alone. How in the hell was she supposed to keep Adam safe and bring him back to Anna?

Adam turned, placed his hands in his pockets, and strolled toward the door. Once inside, he crossed the room and emptied his pockets into a small dish sitting on a bedside table. He removed his weapon from his shoulder harness, released the clip, and placed them in the top drawer.

Calista swallowed a lump in her throat. His methodical movements indicated she was watching a nightly ritual. Last week, her most involved thought regarding Adam Blake was to wonder casually where he went when he left the diner. Now, she was sharing a bedroom with him.

"You must be exhausted," he said. His gaze settled on the bed. "I hope you don't mind sharing a room. I haven't furnished the other rooms yet. You're welcome to the bed."

"Where will you sleep?"

"I've been trained to sleep anywhere. I'll be fine on the sofa."

"The bed is huge, plenty of room for both of us."

Her own words sounded strained to her ears as warmth flushed through her. She turned away from him and began to tidy up a few toiletries she'd used during her shower.

An arm came around her waist. She let out a breath she didn't know she held and eased back against Adam, allowing his warmth and earthy scent to enfold her. Calista turned and placed her arms around him and rested her head on his shoulder. Before she could stop herself, she said, "I made this so much harder for you, Adam. I'm so sorry."

He lowered his head and caressed her lips with his. "When I'm working something out in my head, I get quiet. I'm not angry you are here, Calista. Please believe that." He gaze scanned the room. "I bought this place a couple months ago. It's the prettiest beach I have seen anywhere. I just wish I could have brought you here under much different circumstances."

"Will Ludis follow you here?"

Adam shook his head. "There is nothing that can connect me to this place. And before you ask, we were not followed."

"Then why are you so tense?" she asked, running her hand over the back of his neck and shoulders.

His stare bore into her before he answered. "My uncle will give me the opportunity to locate the disk. While I'm here, he will search for a link that will bring me to him."

Calista sucked in a quick breath. "The McNeils are all protected, right? You wouldn't have left Anna with them if she weren't safe. So what else can Ludis threaten you with?"

Adam released his hold on her and moved to close the French doors, setting the lock in place. With his back still to her he said, "You and your family, Calista."

His ramrod straight posture sent Calista's heart into her stomach as her pulse raced in her veins. "But he doesn't know who I am."

"I have men watching the diner and your grandfather's home." He glanced at his watch. "After a couple hours sleep, I'll visit the unit where I stored away my parents' belongings."

"And if you don't have the disk?"

"We will cross that bridge when we get to it. You said my mother is speaking to my daughter. If that's true, there has to be a way out of this."

Calista searched his eyes. The longing in his expression touched a place deep inside her. She understood this wall. The need to shield Adam from what he faced overwhelmed her. Ludis couldn't win. In the end, the good guys always came out on top, right?

"Just tell me what I can do for you," she whispered.

"Don't die. It will kill the last bit of humanity in me, Calista. I will turn into what I hate about Ludis."

She crossed the room and allowed her fingers to caress the soft stubble down the side of his face to his jaw. "You have more humanity in your fingertip than most men have in their entire bodies. There is so much good in you, Adam. Why don't you see it?"

"You don't know me."

Calista let out a noisy sigh. "I have witnessed in the last few hours what you believe is the real you. That's bull crap." She wadded a chunk of his shirt in her fist. "You did what you had to do to protect your daughter and yourself from Ludis, but that's not who you are."

Adam took her into his arms and pulled her against his chest. "Then who am I? What do you see in me? Why did you get back on the damn plane?"

Calista couldn't form a thought, much less articulate what she wanted to say. Adam's life was hell, and he allowed that hell to define him. He didn't believe he deserved love.

"I got back on the plane to remind you that you had something to live for." She moved her lips over his, drawing him so close that their bodies became one.

He didn't just return the kiss, he consumed her. When her knees began to buckle, he lifted her so they were eye to eye. His other hand tangled in the hair at her neck.

God she needed him, *all of him*.

Adam drew Calista's legs into his arms and laid her gently down on the bed, lowering himself next to her. Breaking the kiss, he studied her for several moments before he spoke.

"You play dirty, Calista Martin."

"At the rectory, you were ready to hand over your life to take down Emil and Ludis. I didn't know what to say to stop you because I'm totally out of my league."

"That's not what I … "

"You practically signed your own death certificate. Since then, I have had time to muck it around in my brain. I can't stop you from going after Ludis by yourself, but I can give you something to live for."

"You can do so much better …"

She held her finger over his lips. He brought it into his mouth. She couldn't keep the whimper from escaping her throat when he moved his mouth over her finger and sucked.

His cobalt eyes swept over her. "What do you want from me?"

"Tonight."

He rose onto his elbow and his hungry stare gripped hold of her heart. Heat began to rise up her neck and into her cheeks.

"You are not some sacrificial piece of meat on a stick, Calista. If all you want is sex…"

Calista cut his tirade with another kiss. He dropped back onto the mattress, pulling her over him as he cradled her head in his hand. As always, the damn man took over, driving her into a sensual whirlpool. She forced herself to break the kiss and yanked back.

"Idiot! How can such an intelligent man be so stupid? I'm not bargaining with sex to keep you alive." She balled her hand into a fist and punched him in the shoulder.

He grabbed her hand in his. "That hurt," he hissed.

"Good. Next time you say something so damn asinine, I'll break something hard over your stubborn, obstinate head."

He let out a laugh and kissed her, hard. "Your eyes are damn beautiful when they are spitting fire."

She sucked in a breath and tried to gain some control of her temper. He hadn't seen anything yet. Just wait until he pissed her off enough that her blood boiled. She brushed her hair from her face and exhaled and studied him for several heartbeats before she said, "Why is it so wrong for me to care about you?

"You can do a lot better than me, Calista."

She reached out to punch him again, but he caught her fist in his hands and brought it to his chest, kissing the knuckles.

"If you knew the things I have done—I will tarnish your life, turning it into the mess I live."

"Are you talking about Rina?"

He nodded.

"Will you tell me about you and Rina?"

"Now? Here?"

Calista could only shrug. She expected Adam to move off the bed and slide the walls back in place, shutting her out. It surprised the hell out of her when he began to speak.

"My greatest sin with Rina is I loved her but never was in love with her. She was my friend, my partner in the field, saved my ass more times than I can count, and was the only person who knew all my shit and loved me anyway."

Adam released Calista's hands and eased off her. He turned onto his back, resting his head on the pillows. He didn't say anything for a long time.

"And?"

Adam turned his head and held her gaze. "I broke her heart."

That was it, nothing more, no explanation. Calista wanted to shove him, poke him, do something to make him start talking again. Waiting as long as she could stand, she said, "Please don't stop there, Adam."

He took in a noisy breath and exhaled. "Our new lives gave us a chance to start over, be new people. Rina wanted the whole picket fence, marriage, happily-ever-after."

"You said you loved her. Why couldn't that work? You, Rina, and Anna could have ... "

"Because it wasn't what I wanted, Calista. I'm a selfish bastard, don't you see? I loved Rina, loved Anna more than I ever knew a person could love another, but I wanted justice—revenge—more than love."

"I don't understand."

"We had a chance to get out of the violent cycle, but I couldn't let go. Emil and Ludis Vasnev were still out there, living high on the hog from the misery of so many."

"But you no longer had the CIA behind you, nor any law enforcement agency to back you up. How could you ..."

"Calista, it was what I had spent the last decade training to do. One man, without the confines of government bureaucracy, can be lethal on his own. I went after the Vasnevs with a vengeance."

"And Rina?"

Adam shifted until his back was against the headboard. The stillness in the room made Calista want to fidget, but she remained calm. When he did finally speak, his voice filled the quiet space with raw grief.

"Rina loved me so much, she gave up her life to protect our child even though she knew I could never be the man she needed. Before Anna, I agreed to leave her alone, give her a chance to find the kind of love she deserved. But hours after Anna was born, I had to see my only child just once. Biggest mistake I ever made."

"Adam, that wasn't a mistake."

"If I never went to that hospital nursery, I never would have known what I was missing. The first time I fell head-over-heels in love was with an infant that weighed all of seven pounds. Anna changed my world, changed my soul." His pain filled eyes held hers. "If I had walked away and left them alone like I promised, Rina would be alive, probably married to a good man, raising her child in a wonderful, loving world free of people like Emil, Ludis ... and me."

He shut his eyes and Calista didn't move. He believed every word he said, which tore her heart in two. He was trying to protect her from *him*.

A tear spilled down her cheek and she quickly swiped it away. She leaned over and placed a kiss at the spot she struck moments before. The next kiss landed on his neck and she worked her way up the side of his face.

"Don't compare yourself with Ludis and Emil again. When I get pissed, I tend to strike out." Balancing herself over him, she circled his neck. "Finding love is a blessing, Adam. Being able to love is why we are all here."

"Calista, ... "

"You were not ready to give Rina what she needed. If that is a sin, then you need to find a way to forgive yourself." She swallowed a sob and continued. "You are one of the most amazing men I have ever known, but you see yourself as a beast." She brushed a strand of hair from his forehead. "I will never be able to make you see the Adam Blake I know. That is someone you are going to have to meet and get to know on your own."

Calista shut her eyes and tried to stop the tears. They never helped in the least. She had a decision to make. Could she accept only the part of Adam he was willing to share?

Opening her eyes, she met his hungry gaze, and took a crazy leap of faith. "I just want tonight. If there is no tomorrow for us, then I don't want to look back and wish ..."

Calista choked on her own words. No future with Adam hurt like hell. "You can send me anywhere you want in the morning. This time I promise to stay away."

Chapter Eighteen

Temptation curled through Adam's gut, driving heat in all the places that mattered. The world of his dreams slammed right into his reality.

Adam rolled Calista under him. She intertwined her legs with his.

"You see, we fit," she said in a hushed tone.

Her sultry expression was one he had never seen before. Panic charged through him. She had no idea what she was doing to him.

Her body squirmed under him, sending a shock of need right to his core. Damn she was good. He should just take what he wanted for once.

And how he wanted his mouth on the perky breasts pressing against his chest. Hell, he wanted to taste every damn inch of her. Adam lowered his mouth and gently caressed her lips with his tongue. Her breath hitched.

"You really want this, Calista?"

"Yes, hell yes!"

The beast she called him earlier burst free and he covered her mouth with his. Calista's taste and the wild, spicy scent from her bath sent him over the edge. When she circled her arms around his neck and wiggled her body against his, he shuddered and gave into the burning need.

He released her mouth and yanked his shirt over his head. He ached for the moment where skin met skin. As if reading his mind, Calista reached for the hem of her t-shirt.

"No, mine," he ordered, and captured her hand above her head. His hands trembled as he moved the hem up over her breast. She wasn't wearing a bra. Thank God! He had never seen anything so beautiful, soft, alluring. With a final tug, he pulled the t-shirt over her head and tossed it across the room.

Did he have a point of no return? It had never happened before, but with Calista anything was possible.

"Adam?"

His name came out in a breathless whisper. He closed his eyes and tried to control his beating pulse. "I want this, Calista. I want you. Damn it to hell, I don't want to stop."

"Who is asking you to?" Her hands spread over his shoulders to his pecs, then down to his waist. "Just this once, will you please stop trying to protect, and take what you want. I need you, Adam."

She moved her hand down to the bulge in his pants. He arched his back as every muscle tensed. Adam flipped the button at the waist of his jeans and yanked down the zipper. He captured her mouth with his as he rolled them onto his side. One more yank and a kick, and his jeans hit the floor.

Calista broke the kiss and ducked her head, taking his left nipple into her mouth. She pushed him onto his back and kissed her way across his chest to the right nipple. The air in Adam's lungs began to burn. Two could play this game.

Adam moved her hands behind his neck. He rose and took a soft, rose peak into his mouth as his hand moved to the waistband of her sweats. She had knotted the string on his old pair so they fit her narrow waist after her shower, but he had no problem finding his way beneath them.

The moment his hand caressed over her mons, Calista rubbed herself against his hardness as if she couldn't get enough of the feel of him. The control he was trying so hard to hang onto faltered. He jerked the sweats off her and sent them flying. He lifted his head and took her mouth for another hard, carnal kiss while his callous hands roamed every inch of her.

Adam lifted her up onto his lap, bringing them chest-to-chest. Again she met him by circling his neck, arching into him. He released her mouth and brought his lips down on her right breast, savoring the taste of her.

Calista gasped and a deep, primal groan made him close his eyes in pure pleasure. He raised his head and met her hungry gaze. She grasped both of his hands in hers and brought them between them.

"Calista, why are you holding my hands?"

"It's so ... I can't breathe."

He never heard that tone in her voice. "Do you want me to stop?"

Calista jerked her head back and forth.

"Sweetheart, I can stop if you want."

Adam watched for several seconds while her gaze scanned the room.

"What the hell are you looking for?" He couldn't keep the harshness from his voice.

"Something to slam over your head."

Adam let out a bark of laughter.

She lowered her lips on his, caressing his bottom lip. "I was just catching my breath. I've never felt anything so ... "

"Intense, powerful?"

"Yeah, but I don't want you to stop."

In one swift move, Adam rolled them both until she perched over him, his body flat on the bed. He brought his hands and intertwined them behind her neck. "Okay, sweetheart. I'm all yours. Take what you want, as fast or slow as you want."

Her hands shook as she caressed the cord of his neck and the down the length of his abdomen. He almost lost it completely when her breasts eased over him, so soft, so feminine.

Her eyes found his. "You are so damn beautiful. I know men don't like that word, but there is none other."

He kissed her and said, "So are you, Calista. Damn beautiful, inside and out. That's rare in my world."

A trail of sweet, intoxicating kisses rained down his jaw line to the tender area just below his ear. As she savored the sensitive skin, her knee moved over his core. A bolt of sheer pleasure shot through his spine to his groin. He pressed into her as his hands grabbed her hips. He wanted her to have the control, to go at her own pace, but her every move was slowly killing him.

If he had a death wish like Calista accused him of, this was the way he wanted to go. His hand moved down her spine, over the silky skin of her cheeks, then around her waist. When his fingers touched her center, his mind reeled.

The moment her thighs widened, Adam fought for control for two seconds, then gave in. Before Calista could take a breath, he pinned her beneath him. An instant later, he drove home and discovered something else that was sorely lacking in his life: Calista Martin.

Chapter Nineteen

A light sea breeze swirled around Calista, sending loose strands of hair into her face. Flipping the hair out of her eyes, she raised her face to the mid-morning sun. The warmth only enhanced her feeling of absolute contentment. Without peering into a mirror, she would bet her last dollar that her skin glowed and she wore the silliest of grins.

If ever there were a perfect moment, she was living it. Waking in Adam's arms after hours of the most intimate, intense lovemaking was a feeling that would live with her the rest of her life.

She glanced down at the row of storage units and peered at a speck of the ocean. If she was very still, she could even hear the waves breaking and the shrill of the seagulls as they searched for their next meal.

Calista turned and watched Adam raise the door of the unit. His muscles bunched in his back and shoulders from the weight of the door. Allowing her gaze to travel down the length of him, she couldn't keep the smile from her lips. She knew what was beneath those tight, black denim jeans.

"Calista?"

"Yes," she hummed.

"Cut it out." Adam drew her against him and kissed the tip of her nose. "You keep looking at me like that and we will be right back where we were only an hour ago. There's work to do." He ran his finger over her lower lip. "Then we can play."

A hot flash of heat rose into her cheeks. She stared into the storage unit. "I have no idea what you are talking about, Adam."

Calista shot him a smile, then flicked on the light switch. Her gaze scanned the mound of boxes stacked in neat rows. A light, powdery dust covered most of the surfaces. Doing a rough count, she came up with about twenty-five boxes all the same size. For some reason, she expected the unit to be jam-packed.

"When was the last time you were here?"

"Ten years."

"I assumed you never went back to your home after they died."

Adam placed an arm around Calista and eased her against him. "It's okay."

Finding her voice, she said, "I was just wondering how you got their stuff out of the house."

"I hid in the woods for hours unable to move. I eventually found the car that Annija hid for me and drove home. I waited outside for a couple hours, then pulled into the garage. I threw some things I thought they would want me to hold onto into boxes," he swallowed hard, "like they were going to come back somehow and want their stuff."

"Oh, Adam."

He rubbed his hand up and down her back as if to comfort her when he was the one who was left on his own with no one to help him deal with his loss.

"I loaded the car and drove away. After driving north for a couple hours, I pulled over and called the police from a pay phone. The thought it could be days until anyone found my parents ... my disappearance is still an open case."

"Did the police think you killed them?"

"No. My parents' time of death was in the time frame while I was in school. The police believe that whoever killed them kidnapped me." Adam stepped back and scanned the small space. "I rented this storage unit right before I entered boot camp. Over the next few years, I stored things here. I guess this place became my home base."

He lugged a couple boxes out of the way as he moved toward the back of the unit. "We only need to search the boxes against the back wall. I'll start on the far left and you can take the right side. We can meet in the middle."

A heart-wrenching pain clutched her. This space was all that was left of two people who loved and raised Adam. There should be more ... stuff.

Calista wasn't sure which hurt more, the fact that a young, innocent, eighteen-year-old was forced to deal with such a tragic loss alone, or that in order to survive, Adam closed himself off from the few reminders of his childhood. An arm came around her middle. Adam stilled her neck and brought his lips down for a quick, tender kiss.

"It's just stuff, Calista."

"No, it's more than that." She tugged the tape off the box nearest her and flipped the lids back. The box was filled with books and several popular board games. She reached in and chose *The Hobbit*.

"These are memories, Adam. Cherished reminders you may want to pass down to Anna." She held his gaze for several seconds. "Does being here after Rina ... "

He cut her off with another kiss.

"I can't go there. Not today."

"Of course." She hugged Adam hard, stepped away, and began to flip through the pages of the book.

Adam moved her back into his arms. "I don't mean to sound callous or unfeeling."

"I know." Calista fingered his jaw. "I understand. You're compartmentalizing."

"You know what you're looking for?"

"Yes, a plastic disk about an inch thick, three inches wide, and five inches long." Her eyes searched the space. "If it's in these boxes, we will find it." She pressed her lips on his neck just below his ear then began pulling out books from the box.

Little was said during the next half hour as Calista flipped through each book and examined the contents of every board game. Resealing the box, she opened the one under it. Tearing back the lid, she let out a gasp. A photo of a beautiful baby boy framed in the center of the cover stared back at her.

Adam's baby album.

In order to remove the album from the box, Calista had to first dig out a smaller album tucked into a corner. After a quick glance at Adam, she eased down onto the concrete floor. Resting her back against the stack of boxes, she began to move slowly through each page. The album was the first year of Adam's life and his parents took great pains in labeling each photo. Annija may have handed her only child over to strangers, but his adoptive parents loved him as if he were their own child.

Setting the album on the top box of the stack next to her, she reached in for another book. In total, there were eighteen full albums, all recording Adam's day-to-day life as he grew to manhood. It took her a half hour to look through each album. Placing them back in the box, she grabbed it, and headed toward the car.

"What are you doing?"

"This one is going with us."

Adam pinned her with a shrewd gaze. "Why? It's just a box of photos."

"You are such a man, Adam Blake." Calista let out an exasperating sigh. "They are not just a bunch a photos. Your parents took great care saving these wonderful memories of your childhood for you. If anything, you need to share this part of your life with Anna."

"As long as it's only one box, Calista," Adam said, breaking eye contact to return to examining the contents of the box in front of him.

After placing the box in the back seat of the car, Calista went back to work. On the top of her own stack of boxes was the small photo album she had dug out of the corner of the previous box. In the center of the cover was a handwritten dedication: *Our greatest joy, the gift of our child.*

After skimming quickly through the book, Calista rose, her stomach in knots. "I think I found something."

Adam set the box he just lifted back on the stack. "What?"

"I think this album was a gift to your mother from your parents." She handed it to Adam.

His eyes narrowed and his features took on a haunted expression.

"Have you ever seen the album before?"

"My mother was making that album for Annija right before she died. I was about to graduate from high school." He reached into his sport coat and retrieved the photo he had shown his father the day before. "I took the photo from the book to have something of Annija with me and stuck the album in the box." He flipped through the first few pages. "I forgot about it."

For the next several moments, Calista studied Adam as he eased each photo out one at a time. A half smile appeared as he reached the last page. Closing the album, he handed it back to Calista.

"No disk."

"Don't you want to hold onto it? It's filled with photos of you with Annija and your parents."

Before Adam could answer, a shadow appeared across the entrance of the unit. Two large men pointed some kind of shotgun at Calista. Adam grabbed her arm and pulled her behind him. He had his weapon out from under his coat and aimed at the men before Calista could even draw a breath.

"Ours are bigger, Blake. Drop your weapon and kick it over to me," one of the men ordered. "Those boxes aren't going to stop ammo piercing rounds."

"Not fucking happening."

The hard edge to Adam's voice sent a chill down Calista's spine while her breakfast did somersaults in her stomach. To give him room, she backed against the back wall. She quickly scanned the area around her but found nothing that could be used as a weapon. Another man appeared in the doorway. His shoulders were so huge he blocked the glare of the sun. In his hands was a familiar plastic gasoline canister. *Holy shit, they were going to burn the place down.*

With a nod from his companion, he removed the cap and began dousing the boxes and doorway with gasoline.

"What the fuck do you assholes want?" Adam took an angry step forward.

An instant later, three large blasts vibrated off the walls. The slugs slammed into the brick inches from Calista's head. Her stomach pitched and fear slithered down her spine. *Oh my God. Oh my God ...*

"You know what we are after. Give us the disk."

"I don't have the fucking disk. I've never had it. Whatever my uncle is paying you, I'll triple it. Just get out of here."

Calista peered through the boxes at the man's reaction. His eyes narrowed and sneered.

"Then you are useless to us."

He nodded to his friend, who splashed gasoline over the front entrance, then shot the lock off the storage unit next door. He made sure to dump the last dregs from the container into that unit before he tossed the can inside their neighboring shed. Then he pulled out a lighter.

Adam fired off a shot. "Ignite it and you're a dead man."

The thug laughed. "You are such a cocky bastard, Blake." He nodded to the other unit. "Don't you want to know what is stored right next to you?" He let out another laugh, gave the lighter a flick with his thumb, and tossed the flame into the unit next to Adam. "If I were you, I would duck."

Calista couldn't see the spark, but the whoosh that instantly followed was very clear. Adam reached back for her arm and shoved her to the ground in the opposite corner of the room. When she hit the concrete, a groan slipped through her lips as a sharp pain shot up her elbow. His body slammed down hard onto hers and his arm covered her head. She tilted her head just in time to see the men run out of view. She began to squirm under the weight, but Adam didn't budge. Just as she opened her mouth to yell at him, a loud blast erupted in the next unit, shaking the ground. Adam's arms tightened over her head, cutting off any air as a scorching heat spread over them.

Calista peered out from under Adam's arm and gasped. The entire front of the unit was one huge ball of fire. She bucked her hips, trying to get his weight off her. "We have to get out of here."

"Wait," Adam roared.

The second the words were out of his mouth, something else exploded next door, spraying chunks of concrete over them. The force of the blast slammed Adam's forehead hard into the back of Calista's head and her chin hit the concrete. The metallic taste of blood spread into her mouth as she choked back a cough.

Adam hauled her to her feet. He yanked his jacket off, drew her to him, and placed the jacket over their heads. Calista's lungs burned from the heat and smoke each time she tried to gasp a breath of air.

"We have to get through the flame," Adam said, with his mouth next to her ear. "Keep your head down. I'll get you out. Move on three."

Calista shot a glance at the entrance. "Wait."

"Damn it, Calista."

She bent and grabbed the small album from the debris and tucked it under her arm.

"We have to go now!"

"Three!" Calista cried out, sucking in a smoke-filled gulp of air. Adam kicked the boxes out of his way and raced through the flame. The intense heat slammed into Calista. She held her breath and shut her eyes.

It took only seconds to clear the flames. Adam tugged her behind him, the heat of the fire hot on her bare neck and arms. He searched the road with his gun ready, but the men had disappeared. With his arm still dragging her with him, he charged toward the car.

"What the hell is stored in that unit?"

Adam peered into the opening. "Fireworks, boxes and boxes of fireworks."

A whistling shrill hit Calista's ears. She glared at Adam.

"Shit! Run!"

Adam grabbed her hand and they dashed across the road just as a hot, flash of air whooshed from the unit followed by an earsplitting explosion. A gust of piercing, hot air lifted them both off the ground and sent them flying into the middle of the street.

Calista held out her hands, knowing they wouldn't lessen the contact to the hard asphalt. As her body slammed to the ground, the last ounce of air escaped her lungs. Pain shot down her arms to her hands as tiny, loose rocks sliced into her palm.

A high-pitched ring drummed between her ears. It took several seconds for her mind to function. Calista rolled onto her back and let out a painful groan. She eased her head up and searched for Adam. He laid only inches from her, unmoving.

God, Adam!

Lifting herself onto her hands and knees, she crawled the short distance, and eased down next to Adam's face. His eyes were closed and blood drained from his nose and mouth.

"Adam?"

Touching the side of his neck, she let out a heavy sigh of relief when his pulse bounced against her fingers. She laid a hand gently against his cheek. In a breathless whisper, she called out to him again as tears burned her eyes. "Please, Adam, say something."

"Fuck," he moaned as his hand covered the hand over his face. He rolled over and sat up, drawing her into his lap. His hands roamed over her head, face and arms.

"Are you okay?"

"I think so." She took in a deep breath of air. "It just hurts everywhere."

Adam rose, pulling her up with him. Calista's knees wobbled. She reached for Adam's arm until she found her balance.

"The damn ringing won't stop," she said, tapping and pulling on her earlobes as her gaze settled on the scorched units.

"We have to get out of here," Adam said, again tugging on her hand.

"Wait."

"Can't. Police."

"What police?" Calista tried to get her feet to cooperate.

Adam didn't slow down to explain. He charged toward the passenger side of the sedan. The windshield was in shards over the dash and front seat, but the rest of the vehicle looked untouched. In less than thirty seconds, they were back on the highway. Calista watched as fire response vehicles turned into the driveway of the storage facility. After several blocks, Adam entered the expressway.

"Where are we going?"

"I haven't figured that out yet."

Calista glanced down at her hands, the cuts and scrapes beginning to burn. She picked out a tiny piece of asphalt from her palm. "Can we go back to the beach house?"

"No."

"The plane?"

"Calista, we can't go back, period. If they found us at the storage unit, Ludis knows my fucking life story."

Calista cringed and struggled to draw in a breath of clean air. Her lungs were raw, her nostrils filled with the acid stench of soot. After letting out a racking cough, she whispered. "I don't understand."

"Someone is feeding Ludis information on me. We are on our own."

"Not your brothers. They wouldn't do that."

Anger ripped through his muscles, the pulse in his neck looked as if it wanted to burst through the skin. "No, not my brothers, but Emil must have had someone very close to him who is now sucking up to Ludis."

Adam's words finally hit home. Gut-wrenching fear ripped through Calista. Everything in the storage unit was gone. There was no disk, the only thing Adam could use to fight this nightmare.

"Why don't they just leave you alone? You don't have the disk and nothing to hold over Ludis's head."

Adam went still. The silence between them only revved up the panic building in Calista.

He finally cleared his throat and said, "Ludis knows me. I will never let him go free. I couldn't save Annija or Rina, but I will take care of Ludis."

"Then why look for the disk if you are just going to … "

"Calista, with the disk, there may have been a way to take him down without crossing *that* line."

Her mind reeled, gasping for some kind of solution. This was so far out of her experience, she had no idea what to do next. Without the disk, Adam and Anna would never be safe. And where did that leave the McNeil family?

She circled her waist with her arm to worn off the chill that settled deep in her spine. A thick substance coated her arm right below the elbow. She raised it and swallowed hard as the pain from her side cursed through her.

"Adam," she moaned.

He skirted around traffic then turned to her. Shock slowly seeped into his every feature. "Oh shit. Where are you hurt?"

"My right side." She set her hand on the area as the pain began to burn through her. "It's just a scratch."

He lifted her hand. It was covered with blood. "Does this look like just a scratch?"

His foot hit the accelerator and he raced across four lanes of traffic, leaving behind honking horns and screeching brakes. He exited the freeway and drove down the access road, turning into the parking lot of a large shopping mall. Finding an isolated spot, he slammed the car in park and got out. He charged around the sedan, threw open the passenger side door, and knelt down.

"Calista, move your hand so I can see." Adam's voice was gentle, but his eyes had transformed to pools of black. He eased up her stained t-shirt and sucked in air. "Shit!" He shook his head. "It's deep."

He used the edge of her shirt and gently dug out something in the cut. It hurt like crazy, but Calista clenched her jaw tight to keep from moaning.

"There are pieces of the cement block still in the wound," he said, fingering the blood-covered piece of mortar between his thumb and forefinger. Wiping it off on his jeans, he cupped his hand around her neck, and brought his lips down on the top of her head. "I'm sorry, Calista, so sorry."

"Don't, Adam," she choked out. "This isn't your fault."

"Like hell it isn't. I should have kicked you off the damn plane and cuffed you to the inside of Jared's truck." He swept a hand over his face and let out a noisy sigh. "I need to get you to a hospital."

"No, you are not dumping me alone in some strange emergency room, damn it."

A sob clogged Calista's throat and she couldn't keep the tears away. She was more frightened than she could ever remember in her life, but the thought of being without Adam left her empty. "Can't you clean the wound, close it up?" She hitched in a painful breath and swallowed. "Like Jason Bourne. He patched up his wounds."

"Who the hell is Jason Bourne?"

"Forget it. You can do something, right?"

"I need supplies, drugs … "

"We can stop at the pharmacy. Maybe Mary McNeil can call in something."

He didn't answer right away. A mixture of longing, doubt, and fear settle deep within her. She didn't want to add to Adam's problems, but she couldn't allow him out of her sight either. Anna's words swam around her head.

If you don't go with Daddy, I'll never see him again.

What if there was some scheme in play where she played the leading role of keeping Adam alive? She couldn't do that in a hospital bed.

"Adam?"

He let out a string of curse words then yanked out his cell, punching a number on speed dial. "I need a favor, a huge favor."

Chapter Twenty

With a foot on the brake, Adam slowly eased into the rutted parking lot of a nameless hotel. The heat radiating off the asphalt began to seep through the cracks, turning the interior into an oven the moment he shut off the ignition. Rolling his shoulders, he eased his t-shirt off his clammy back, and scanned the rugged terrain. The small, dusty town off the main highway in Death Valley was the perfect place to lay low for the next twelve hours. After a much needed shower to wash off the grime and soot, he was going to shut it all off and give himself time to recharge.

How had Ludis discovered the storage unit? The place was rented under an alias and there was nothing in the paperwork that could be tied back to Adam. He had left anything that could be traced electronically in the hotel room with Calista's belongings right after Ludis blew up Rina's home. As for his vehicle, he removed the tracking device himself. Yet somehow, his uncle's men not only found out about the storage unit, but came prepared to torch him into an early grave.

Adam glanced at Calista who laid prone in the passenger seat. The gash on her right side wasn't as serious as he first thought. After a quick stop for supplies, he cleaned and dressed the wound. There were other scrapes and burns he would take care of when they stopped for the night. She dozed off into a restless sleep once they were back on the highway.

His brothers came through for him in a big way. Noah organized sleeping accommodations while Jared arranged for someone he trusted to charter a plane outside of Las Vegas for a flight back to Maryland. At this point, Calista's safety was his highest priority.

In the last sixteen years, he learned how to take care of himself and those he cared about. He had been in some horrifying situations, but he somehow maintained the upper hand. Nothing in his past came close to the mess he was in now. If there was a way out, he couldn't see it, and that scared the shit out of him.

The only way he could insure everyone's safety was to force Ludis to confess his involvement. For that, he needed the disk, which if existed in the first place, was now a melted wad of crap on the floor of his storage unit.

Adam had only one option. He had to kill Ludis. Going against a man in Ludis's position was a death sentence, but his family would be safe. Of course, Anna would grow up without him in her life, and Calista …

Hell, he couldn't do that to either one of them or himself. He killed on the job. He wasn't a murderer.

Adam opened the driver's door and eased his sore, stiff body out of the car. After another quick scan of the area, he rolled the tension from his muscles and unlocked the trunk. The entrance to his motel room was only a few feet from the parking lot.

Using the room card, he unlocked the door, and a blast of cool, clean, fragrant air filled his nostrils. He dumped the contents of the bags onto the far side of the king bed. Returning to the car, he opened the passenger door, knelt, and lightly stroked Calista's cheek with his thumb. Like him, soot covered her face, neck, and arms while angry scrapes covered her elbows and hands. Her bloodstained clothing was ripped to shreds and beyond repair.

Adam rubbed a rough hand over his face and silenced the string of curse words flooding through his head. He was better than this. What the hell happened to his training the last few hours?

"Stop it, Adam," Calista said in a hoarse whisper. "You're doing that blame thing again and it's pissing me off."

"Can't," he replied and tried to plant a smile on his face. "We have a place to stay for a few hours. Can you move?"

"Yes." She tried to sit up, but her face distorted with pain.

"Stop. I'm going to carry you, Calista. It's going to hurt the gash on your side like a motherfu…

"Just do it, I'll be fine."

Removing the seatbelt, he twisted to face her. He placed one hand behind her back and the other one under her knees. He lifted her against his chest, carefully clearing her feet from the door. Using his hip, he slammed it shut, locked it with the key fob, and hurried into the room.

"Not on the bed," Calista forced out the minute he closed the motel door.

"Then where?"

"I need to clean off the soot first."

Adam headed into the small restroom. He set Calista back onto her feet. Her hand never left her side as she took a moment to find her balance.

"Just lean against me, sweetheart, and let me help you," he said as he turned the water on at the sink then grabbed the towels and washcloths off the rack.

She rested her head against his chest and met his gaze in the mirror. "I'm fine, Adam." She raised her hands. "I'm a natural-born klutz. I do this much damage just riding my bike back and forth to school and the diner."

She placed her hands under the warm water and began to wash the grime and blood from her palm. Closing her eyes, tears glistened on her eyelashes as she took in deep, cleansing breaths.

Adam wrapped his arm around her front and held her. "Shit," he said under his breath. He moved her hands from the water and pressed the hand towel to her palms as gently as he could. "What else hurts?"

"My elbows," she whispered.

She reached for the hem of her shirt and pulled it over her head. Adam bit back a string of profanity when he saw the condition of her arms and elbows. The blast from the second explosion left third degree burns on her left shoulder. A long, angry scrape began at her elbows and extended down to her wrist.

"I have something that will help with the pain," he said, and headed back into the room. He grabbed the open box of gauze, ointment, and tape. Calista stood completely still as he gently washed each abrasion, applying a healthy amount of ointment, and wrapped her arm from her elbow to the wrist with the gauze.

He turned her so she faced him. "Where else, Calista?"

"That's it." A small smile graced her lips, but the tears in her eyes tore him in two.

"I wish I had some pain meds."

"I hate taking those things. They make me nauseous."

"I hate you in pain," Adam murmured, lightly brushing her hair off her face. A lone tear escaped down her cheek. Adam lowered his head and caught the tear with his lips. "I will make this up to you."

Calista took his hand in hers and kissed his knuckles. "I don't need that, Adam."

He swallowed hard. "What do you need then?"

"You. I just need you."

Her words pierced through his heart, shattering it into pieces. "Have you looked in the mirror? Why in the hell would you want to be with me?"

Calista studied him for a long time before she spoke. "You know damn well why. You feel it too."

"I'm not good ..."

Calista fisted her hands and slammed them into his chest. "Don't you dare say it!" She let out a heavy sigh. "Sometimes, Adam, you are such a dumbshit. There isn't enough love in the world as it is," she said as she pinned him with a heated glare. "When someone is giving you their heart, you don't stomp on it." She swiped away the moisture on her cheeks. "You accept it, hold it close, cherish it, and never allow anyone to take it from you."

Calista jerked out of his hold and stepped back. "I know what you are doing, Adam Blake, and I will not make this easy for you." She shoved him to the side and stormed out of the restroom.

"And what the hell am I doing?"

"You are going to dump me somewhere and turn yourself over to your uncle."

Adam took hold of her fists and brought them to his lips. It took a moment before he could speak. "I don't think anyone has ever dared call me a dumbshit to my face."

"Get used to it, big guy. It's going to become one of my favorite nicknames for you."

Calista's words trailed off and her eyes closed. She pulled her hand free from his hold and dropped down on the bed.

Adam sat next to her and said in a low whisper, "I don't want to hurt you, Calista."

"Then don't leave, don't do this to your daughter ... and to me. Anna was right all along. You had no intention of coming back to us."

"What the hell are you talking about?"

Calista lowered her head and tightened her arms around her waist.

"I'm waiting, Calista."

She stretched her feet out in front. "Anna told me on the runway in West Virginia that if I didn't come with you, she would never see you again."

So that was why she got back on the damn plane. "There is no way in hell Anna could have known any of this would happen. She just didn't want me alone. That's it."

"I get that she's just a little girl trying to hold onto the only family she knows. But what if she knows something you couldn't possibly know? You are being pigheaded not to consider the possibility."

"Dumbshit and now pigheaded. You sure the hell found yourself a great guy, Calista."

Calista ran a shaky hand through her curls and bit back a sob. "I see you for who you are and want you anyway."

"You don't know what—"

"Seriously, if you don't shut up, I'm going to hurt you. I have something to say, and damn it, you are going to listen."

"So talk."

Calista wiped another tear off her face and stood. Adam let her go. With her back to him, she began to speak. Her voice was filled with so much pain, it cut deep.

"If you didn't want something to develop between us, why didn't you just stay away from me? You had to know how this was going to play out. Did you think you could just disappear out of my life and everything would return to normal as if you never existed?"

For an instant, their gazes held until Calista lowered her eyes, breaking their connection. "I knew you were dangerous from the very first. I moved back with my grandfather because I felt safe there, loved. I needed that to recover after my best friend was murdered."

"Murdered? When the hell ... "

"Hanna Tu was my roommate, my best friend in the world. But you know all that, don't you? That's why you came into the diner that first day. It was to meet me and see if I was a continual threat to your sister-in-law, your family."

Adam stormed back into the room. "No, damn it. That isn't what happened." He could feel the fear in her, how terrified she tried not to act around him. Now he knew why.

Calista glanced down at her feet. Clearing her throat, she faced Adam. "This is why I was so pissed at you at Jared's. When he walked out of the house, and then I met Jennie, everything just clicked. I assumed you ... hell, it doesn't matter anymore. So much has happened since then. It all proves one thing. We are like ice and water. You break through your problems, risking everything for the people you love. I, on the other hand, sink back into the familiar, hiding behind my grandfather's apron, my music, afraid to fight back."

"Shit! Calista. God, I didn't know." He cupped her face in his hands. "I walked into Pete's because I hadn't eaten all day and was starving. I wasn't investigating you."

"I don't believe in coincidences, Adam."

A small smile appeared at the corner of his lips. "Neither do I, but there has been some strange shit going on. Annija talking to Anna, the whole telepathic thing between me and Anna ..."

"You think Annija brought you to the diner?"

Adam shrugged. "Crazy stuff like this doesn't happen in my world. Maybe I've taken a step into the rabbit hole. The idea doesn't sound so crazy anymore."

She took a step back and just stared at him. When she finally spoke, her voice was so faint, Adam almost missed what she said.

"I just wish I had been strong enough to fight this damn pull we have between us now."

"I never meant to do that to you."

The fierce look she fired at him slammed into him like a fist to the gut. "What happened last night meant everything to me. For me to allow someone to get that close, that intimate, there has to be ... I have to be ... damn it, I'm in love with you." She raked a shaky hand through her hair then penned him with a glare. "I'm sure you never meant that to happen either."

Adam dropped down on the edge of the bed. He didn't know how to answer. No, he sure as hell didn't want to hurt another woman like he hurt Rina. He would go to his grave with that on his soul. But he also didn't want to be *that* man anymore either. Adam's future passed before his eyes during Emil's psychotic episode. Unless he stopped the pattern of malice in his life, he would destroy what Annija sacrificed everything for and become the one thing she feared: a carbon copy of Emil and Ludis.

Before he could come up with a reply, Calista pitched a pillow at his face. The second one hit him between his eyes while the third slammed into the side of his head. By the time she was done, all six pillows on the bed were either surrounding him or on the floor while tears streamed down her face.

"From the moment I stepped into the scene in Rina's living room, there was part of you I knew I would never touch, but I allowed myself to fall hard anyway. And as much as I hate the violence in your life you wear like a damn coat, I would have found a way to deal with it because you are worth it."

He stood and took a step toward Calista.

She brought her hands up as if to ward off a blow.

"Stop. Don't touch me. You lost that right with death wish number two." She moved out of reach until her back was against the door.

Adam reached for her and pulled her against him. He held her close until she stopped struggling. "You think this is what I want, Calista? Do you for a second think I don't want to be there beside you, in your arms, in your bed, buried so deep inside you we are one?" He wanted to shake her but instead moved his hands up and laced his fingers around the back of her neck.

"If you were in my shoes, what would you do? We are talking about your life. They will kill you and Anna. I have to stop that from happening."

Calista leaned her head against his chest and whispered, "If you don't come back, I'll know … you sacrificed yourself for me. How in the hell am I'm supposed to get over that, Adam?"

The dam broke and Calista sobbed into his shirt. Seeing the cuts and bruises on her skin was horrible, but nothing in his life had prepared him for what her heartbreaking tears did to him. "Calista, please don't."

"There has to be another way." She grabbed his collar and yanked hard. Taking control, Calista lifted her head. "Annija went to great extremes to keep you safe from her brother. Whether you believe it or not, Anna knows her. Maybe she knew this day would come and planned for it by—"

"Son-of-a-bitch!"

Adam slammed the palm of his hand into the door so hard that it made Calista jump. "What the hell, Adam?"

He then scrubbed his hands over his face. "Say that again."

"What?"

"The part about extremes."

He snatched the car keys off the dresser, lifted Calista away from the door, and opened it. Calista began to follow him, but he yelled out, "Stay inside. I'll be right back."

He charged toward his car and unlocked the passenger side front door. He reached over the front seat for the smaller album. Back inside the room, he drew out his pocket knife and dropped onto the foot of the bed. After flipping through the pages one more time, he drew the blade out of the knife and began scraping back the white cardstock in the front cover until the edges of the glued leather covering were exposed.

"Adam, what are you doing?"

"Finding another way out of this mess." He drew Calista down next to him and kissed her hard on the mouth.

Calista's hand covered his. "We both have been through the album." She ran her hand over the cover. "If there was something hidden behind the cover, you could feel it. There isn't anything there."

"The last time I saw this album it was on the dining room table. My mom used that as her craft center. Ludis would have given the clutter craft table only a momentary glance. But Annija ..."

"Annija what?"

"She would have noticed what my mother was working on."

"I don't understand."

"Annija would have noticed the album and understood its importance to me." A smile spread across his face. "Hiding something in plain sight is the oldest trick in the book."

The leather cover came away easily. Under the cover was a quarter inch piece of cardboard glued to a thicker square. Adam held his hand steady as he ran his knife along the edge. He lifted the sheet and his heart dropped to his stomach. Using the tip of the knife, he raised the cover off a meticulously carved rectangle approximately three inches by five inches in diameter embedded into the cardboard. A thin, white plastic disk sat in the center.

Adam lifted it out and tossed it in the air. Placing an arm around Calista, he brought his lips down on hers. Before his brain became fried by the amazing woman in his arms, he broke the kiss and said, "How about we see what is so damn important on this tape that would drive a man to murder?"

Chapter Twenty-One

The sun dipped beneath the horizon, leaving behind black streaks across the starless sky. Taking in a deep breath of salty sea air, Calista fortified herself with an inter strength she never tapped into before and strolled to the wall of the patio that overlooked the ocean. She peered out at the dark water. Grayish thick storm clouds spread across the moon as the white-capped waves pounded the shore. A storm was rolling in, making the air sticky which only added to the overwhelming gloom that settled deep into every crevasse of Calista's heart.

With the disk in hand, shouldn't she feel elated? Adam had what he needed to keep his family safe. The nightmare should be over.

Except for the sporadic concern for her welfare, any tenderness in him dissolved away the moment he discovered the disk in the album cover. He raised another thick wall around himself, growing very quiet during the drive back to his home outside of Los Angeles. Calista didn't even try to breach it. Not that Adam gave her much of a chance.

Turning toward the house, Calista watched Adam as he paced across the living room floor, talking to one of his brothers. Jared, Noah, she couldn't tell them apart. They were in the air within minutes of Adam's call and arrived about a half hour ago. All three men were in there planning her life, trying to find a place she would be safe while they met with Ludis.

Even with a storm on its way, the air on the patio was much easier to breathe than the air inside. Calista took in another breath and tried to calm down.

Why did they return to the beach house? It was as if Adam was double-dog daring Ludis to come get him. If he was setting a trap, where was his police backup? His brothers were cops. Why not call in LAPD, FBI, swat team … hell, everyone? How were three brothers going to survive against Ludis and his army of goons on steroids?

Calista let out a sign and offered up a prayer for Rina. It was so easy to fall into her footsteps. Annija was with Anna. Adam said no one knew him like the mother of his child. Could Calista use a few of Rina's words of wisdom right about now.

She loved Adam, the whole man, not just a few select parts of him. He didn't see it in himself, but he was a good man who deserved the best in life. If she had to, she would fight for *them*. It was put up or shut up time.

Arms circled her waist and she was drawn back against Adam's hard chest.

"It's going to be okay, Calista. Just have a little faith. It will all work out."

Calista swallowed a lump in her throat. "What do you need me to do? How can I help?"

"This isn't your battle." He gently turned her so they were face to face. "I don't want you anywhere near Ludis."

"Adam, I want to … "

"No, not this time, Calista." He drew her close to him and cupped his hands behind her neck. His eyes glistened as he tried to smile. He brought his lips down on her forehead. "Last night, you promised you would go wherever I asked. Remember?"

She shoved down a sob and nodded.

His arms dropped, circling her waist. He cradled her against him as his fingers played with the curls at her shoulders. With his lips close to her ear, he whispered, "Don't fight me this time. I can't be the man you know right now. I have to focus on ending this nightmare and that requires me to be someone I don't want you to ever meet."

Calista raised her head and didn't hide any of the emotions churning through her. Stroking his cheek, she said, "I already know that man, Adam. He's the same man I met in the diner months ago." She wrapped both arms around his neck, linking her fingers together. "I'll leave, but not because I can't stomach seeing a different side of you. I don't want you to worry about me. It will distract you." She tugged him tight to her chest. "But understand one thing, Adam Blake, if you so much as get an itsy bitsy scratch, I'm going to be royally pissed. You got that?"

Adam's gaze grew intense, his irises turning a deeper shade of blue. His body shook as he lifted her up so they were eye to eye. He brought his lips down inches from hers for an instant then took control completely. The kiss was hard, demanding, but held such promise.

He broke away from her. "Same goes for you, sweetheart." He lightly brushed the gauze wrapped around her arm. "Not one scratch. You keep yourself safe. We have things that need to be said to each other. I heard every word, felt them in my soul. I just couldn't …"

Calista placed two fingers over his mouth. "I should have never thrown that at you while I was upset—hurt." She let out a heavy breath as she allowed herself to be drawn into the intensity of his gaze. "I meant every word. Next time I'll do a better job at expressing myself." Moisture formed at the corner of her eyes and her throat burned. "How in the hell am I supposed to walk away from you when all I want to do is shield you from this damn nightmare?"

"I'm the one that's supposed to fight the monsters back."

"Well, Adam Blake, when one of those monsters threatens the man I love, the fists come out. That's how Pete raised me. You are just going to have to get used to the idea."

Adam let out a deep chuckle and kissed her forehead. "I think I'm going to need a list. Dumbshit, fist-waving she-wolf. Anything else?"

Calista threw her arms around him and hugged him tightly. Her body screamed out to sob like a newborn baby, but she wouldn't do that to Adam. Drawing in his clean, spicy scent, she slid down his chest until her feet settled on the patio tile and took a step away. "No, I think that's it for now."

His brother cleared his throat in the doorway. "We got something," he said with a cell phone to his ear. "Ludis Vasnev just took a room at the Ritz."

"Cocky bastard. Do you have someone on him?"

"My tech guy has logged into the hotel cameras and the traffic cameras around the block. If he leaves, we'll know." He looked pass Adam and met Calista's gaze. "We need to get you out of here. Will you be ready in about five minutes?"

"Yes."

"Jared is going to stay with me," Adam said, nodding toward the brother in the doorway. "Noah is going to stick to you like glue."

"But with Noah with me, that will only leave you and Jared against Ludis. That's crazy."

"This is what I do, Calista, and I'm damn good at it. In this situation, less is more. Trust me."

She could only nod. There were no words in her vocabulary to express what was going through her at that moment. With every bit of strength she could find, she choked down her fear, and took a step out of Adam's arms.

"Then go do what you do best. I'll be ready whenever Noah wants to leave." Wrapping her arms around her middle, she turned back toward the ocean.

He lifted the hair back from her neck, planting a soft kiss right below her right ear. Calista waited to hear him with his brothers before she allowed the tears to fall. She didn't know how long she stood there, but her mind drifted to the moments hours earlier when she woke in Adam's arms.

She felt someone standing off to her side before the sound of his shoes on the gravel hit her ears. She turned expecting to see Noah. Her throat closed up just as she opened her mouth to scream. Ludis Vasnev stood inches from her.

Forcing her feet to move, she bumped into the corner of the patio wall. She grabbed hold of the brick base for balance. "The place is surrounded."

"Liar, liar, pants on fire." He clamped hold of Calista's forearm, and pulled her over the wall as he held a wet, sweet-smelling cloth at her mouth and nose. He swung her like she weighed nothing over his shoulder and ran full out into the trees. She tried to yank out of his hold, but her arms and legs wouldn't move. Just as he disappeared into the trees, nausea roiled in her stomach and then everything went black.

Chapter Twenty-Two

Standing in the doorway of the study, Adam stared at Calista's back. He didn't have to see her tears for them to rip a new hole in his heart. He wasn't *that man* who rinsed and repeated the same damn mistakes over and over again. Calista worked her way under his skin like no other woman, even Rina.

Squaring his shoulders, he joined his brothers at the kitchen bar. He lifted the Ikegami digital recorder out of the box that Jared had retrieved from Adam's storage unit in Maryland. Setting the recorder on the counter, he pressed the reject button and set the disk in the chamber.

"How long have you been hanging onto the recorder?" Noah asked.

"Twelve years. Actually found it at an estate sale. The camera from Annija's car was too damaged in the wreck to be repaired."

"If you knew nothing about your mother's life or what led her to you the day she died, how did you know you would need the camera?"

Adam drew his attention away from Noah, his gaze zeroing in on a speck on the carpet. "There was nothing in the car, no purse, no luggage ... nothing except the recorder," he said in a hoarse whisper. "It was important to my mother. I didn't understand at the time just how important. Ikegami only made fifty of these. Today, it would be almost impossible to find one. It's a technical nightmare to play the tape without it. After we see what is on this sucker, I'm turning it over to the FBI." He faced his brothers. "Do you have a problem with that?"

The twins shared a look. Jared broke the silence that settled over the room. "We can deal with Ludis on your terms. That isn't necessary. You know that, right?"

Adam shifted his feet and planted his fist in his pockets. "I'm tired of being someone else. Who I became … what I had to do to protect Anna I will never apologize for, but that chapter is over. I'll deal with the fallout of faking my own death. I need to be *me* again."

"Does Calista know?"

"No. I guess I was hoping for some kind of miracle, but I think I have been given my share of those. I have to face what's coming and so will Calista … and Anna."

Noah rested his hand on Adam's shoulder. "She's in love with you and this will hurt her."

Hearing the words spoken out loud sent an ache into the pit of his stomach. The last thing he wanted to do was add more heartache to Calista, but Adam had little control over his future.

His eyes searched out the patio door. The area near the wall was empty. He moved toward the door and scanned the yard. "Shit! Calista, where in hell are you?"

He stepped out onto the patio. It was empty. He charged to the wall and glanced down the hill to the beach. It was clear as well.

"Son of a bitch." Adam spun around. "Noah, check the upstairs. Calista isn't out here."

Noah took the steps two at a time. The minute he searched the upstairs was hell on earth. Adam met him at the bottom step. "Well?"

"She's not up here."

"What the fuck." Adam turned and ran out into the yard at the same time as a now familiar piercing pain shot across his forehead. Anna's panicked voice vibrated between his ears.

"Daddy, hurry, the white-haired man is hurting Calista!"

Adam bent low, trying to catch his breath while both hands pressed his temples. Finding his balance, he rushed past Jared. He shoved his Glock into his shoulder harness as he pushed down the fear pulsing through his veins.

"Adam?" Jared placed a hand on his elbow.

"Ludis has Calista."

"How ... "

"Anna just told me." Adam couldn't catch his breath as Rina's lifeless body spread through his mind.

"How in the hell ... "

"I don't know." He headed for the patio. "I'm going after him. There is no sign of anyone on the beach so he had to grab her off the patio and head into the woods."

Jared yanked out his phone. "I'll call for backup. "

"I'm not waiting. Tell them whatever you have to get them here," Adam said, grabbing the collar of his brother's shirt. "And I mean everything, Jared. Got it. Calista's safety is the priority."

"I understand, Adam."

Racing out the patio doors, he leaped over the retaining wall. Once his feet hit the gravel, he ran full out down the hill until he came to the path leading into the woods. He took a moment to scan the area. Rage rippled through him. Closing his eyes, he did something he never had bothered doing before. "What way, Anna? Tell me what way to go."

A calmer, melodic voice answered. *"He's running up, Daddy."*

As soon as the pain from Anna's words eased, he charged across the path for about a mile that ran parallel to the shore until it dead-ended at a small cliff where it split. One path led down to the beach while the other narrower path climbed into the dense forest. Adam didn't waste an instant checking the beach but took his daughter's words to heart and began to climb.

After another couple miles into the dense woods, he stopped, grew very still, and listened to the sounds of the night; the wind shifting through the new leaves, the chirps and movements of the insects rustling in the undergrowth. He calmed his breathing so he could focus on which noises didn't belong.

It didn't take long to extract the mumbled voices due north of him. Adam sprinted down the trail, jumping over decaying logs in his path while trying to duck under low hanging branches. Missing several in the darkness, they slapped against his forehead, cheeks, and forearm.

As the path climbed higher into the woodlands, Adam tried to slam down the panic building in his gut. The only clear thought that kept him from going over the edge was that Ludis took Calista because she was the perfect shield.

A high pitch scream of pain pierced the night. Calista! What was that bastard doing to her?

Before Adam could react, the blast of gunfire echoed off the dense forest wall. Terror sliced across his heart, almost erasing years of combat training. Shoving the emotion deep, he concentrated on allowing the adrenaline pumping through his veins to take over.

Leaping over the shorter bushes that outlined a small grassy area, he came to a dead stop. Steadying his stance, he took aim at Ludis, whose back was facing away from him.

Ludis held his gun stretched out in front of him, his shoulders shaking with fury. Calista stood only a few feet away from Ludis clutching a branch in her hand like a baseball bat. For a moment, neither of them noticed Adam.

"Drop the stick, Calista," Ludis roared, his fury edging on madness.

Great. A stick against a fucking gun. Adam swallowed the bile in his throat.

"Enough, Ludis. It's over. You don't have to hurt her." Adam took an angry step forward. Calista's breathing came in short, raspy breaths. She was scared shitless, but he was damn proud of her for holding her ground.

"Calista, are you all right?"

"Peachy," she hissed, never taking her eyes off Ludis.

He took another step, but stopped dead when Ludis fired off a shot, clipping a chunk from the top of the branch.

"You bastard! You could have hit her."

"I said drop the fucking stick. The next one will be between your eyes, Calista."

The branch hit the ground. Ludis pivoted and shot a glare at Adam. "Your turn, dear nephew," he growled and yanked Calista by her bandaged elbow hard against his chest.

"Adam, don't ... "

Ludis slammed his arm around Calista's throat and squeezed. He backed further away from Adam, dragging Calista with him. She tripped on something in the dark and almost fell, but he hauled her back up by the throat.

"Damn it. Let her go! You're choking her."

"I said drop the gun or I'll snap her pretty little neck."

Pure, undiluted hatred made his head spin. "You win," he said, lowering his gun to the ground. "Let her go."

"Remove the clip and toss it into the bushes."

Adam weighed his options. He still had a knife and a small caliber gun in an ankle holster. Chances of reaching either in time were slim to none.

He quickly removed the clip and hurled both pieces into the night. Dread overwhelmed him, but he kept his face bland as he faced his uncle. He had only one card left to play and it was going to be a hell of a play. Somehow, he had to reason with a cold-hearted killer.

"It's over, Ludis. Just let her go." He took a couple steps toward them.

"Give me the fucking disk first."

"I never even knew the disk existed until two days ago and I don't have it now. Don't make it worse. Just let Calista go and disappear. It's your only chance to live past the night." With his hands in the air, he took another step closer. "All I want is Calista."

Ludis's body trembled, his features distorted with sheer hatred. "And allow you to have everything? Fuck that."

Fear pulsed through Adam. As if in slow motion, he watched Ludis's finger close in on the trigger. Making himself move, he dropped to the ground. At the same time, Calista shot an elbow hard into Ludis's bandaged shoulder. He let out an animalistic howl and stumbled backward.

Adam reached for his second gun and yanked it free. But as he brought it up, he saw Calista had the limb back in her hands. With the skill of a seasoned baseball player, she swung it at Ludis's head, connecting wood to skin right above his right eye. An instant later, Ludis dropped to the ground, out cold.

"Calista," Adam let out in a hoarse whisper as he stumbled to his feet. He didn't even know he moved, but she was in his arms, clutching his neck in a death hold. With his arm around her waist, he leaned down and pressed two fingers against the pulse at Ludis's neck.

"Is he dead?"

"No. The bastard is still breathing." He released her, pulled off his belt and secured Ludis's arms behind his back. He then took Calista back into his arms. "It's over, sweetheart. I got you."

His heart drummed between his ears and he clung to Calista with everything he had in him. Then his lips found hers, and for the first time in years, he allowed the world to slip into oblivion.

Desire slammed into him along with something new and wild. He took everything she offered as the overwhelming fear and desperation he carried with him drained from his body.

Adam broke the kiss and ran his hands down her arms then back up. "Are you all right? Did he hurt you?"

Calista placed her hands over his. "My head hit a branch. It hurts a little but it's just a bump."

Twisting her so he could see the back of her head, he ran a gentle hand down her hair until he felt a large lump below her left ear. It was too dark to see the damage, but the bleeding seemed to have stopped.

"Did you lose consciousness?"

"Yes, but not from the tree that got in the way of my head. Whatever was on the cloth he held over my mouth knocked me out for a couple minutes. I came to on the trail by the cliff. I'm a little nauseous but fine."

"I heard a scream."

Calista covered his mouth with hers, silencing him. The tenderness of the kiss knocked him off balance. She broke away and met his gaze.

"I tried to get away and he yanked me back by my hair. I got free, but when I ran, he fired a shot over my head." She picked up the fallen limb. "That's when I picked up the stick and you know the rest."

Adam drew her back into his arms, holding her so tightly, there wasn't an inch separating them. "I thought ... God, Calista."

A sob burned in the back of his throat and he couldn't find the words. Instead, he cradled her head against his chest as tears blurred his vision.

"I can't lose you, Calista. You understand?" He reached for her hand and placed it against his heart. "You feel the beats?"

She nodded.

"One beat is for Anna, the other one is all you." He wrapped his fingers through her hair. Bringing his head down so it rested on hers, he choked out, "I'm nothing without you."

Several male voices and the glaring beam of flashlights erupted from the trees. Before he could get another word out, several law enforcement officers surrounded them. Adam tucked his arms under her legs and lifted her against him. He stepped over the still unconscious Ludis and headed back across the small clearing.

One of the men wearing an F.B.I. vest approached him. "Adam Blake?"

"Yes."

"You need to come with us."

Adam shoved past him and approached the trail. The man followed, grabbing Adam's arm.

Adam turned and glared at him. "First, I take care of her. Got it?"

This time the man let him go.

Calista placed a hand on his cheek. "I can walk. Seriously, I'm fine, Adam."

He slowed his pace. "I like carrying you. Besides, I'm not letting you out of my sight until a doctor checks out the lump on your head."

"Why did the agent act like he was arresting you?"

Adam couldn't find the words to answer her question. Instead he used all his energy to work his way back down the trail. Lifting her over the wall, he gently set her back on her feet onto the patio. Noah and Jared stood a few feet away with several law enforcement officers.

Jared cleared his throat. "You said call everyone. If there were any other way …"

"It's okay, Jared. You did the right thing." He broke eye contact with his brother and wrapped an arm around Calista. "She was the priority."

She stepped away from him. "Adam, what's going on?"

He swallowed a sob that burned the back of his throat. Pulling her back into his arms, he held her as his mind raced to find the right words. No matter how he said it, it was going to tear them apart.

"The agents are not here just to take Ludis into custody."

"I don't understand. You said it was over. We found the tape and Ludis can't hurt you anymore. What else is there?" With each sentence, the panic in her voice grew.

"Calista, I haven't had a chance to view what's on the disk, but Ludis went to extremes to get his hands on it." When she tried to interrupt, he held up his hand. "It has to be something of great value. Even before he showed up here, I had planned to turn everything over to my brother, Mac, who works with the F.B.I."

"But that doesn't have anything to do ... "

"You do understand what it means for me to turn the disk over, right?" He took a step back, keeping his hands on her waist.

Calista slowly shook her head as everything became clear. Adam tugged her closer and tried to calm his voice. "I was a federal agent who five years ago faked my own death."

She took in a shaky breath as her eyes darted to the men standing near Jared and Noah. "No, Adam, damn it, we can just leave. Now!"

"I pretended I was kidnapped by insurgents. The military sent men into the area to rescue me."

Calista dropped her arms and stepped back. "But you were protecting Rina and Anna. You didn't profit from pretending to be dead, right?"

"It's still fraud, sweetheart. I have a lot to answer for."

"Did your brothers turn you in?"

Adam raked both hands over his face and met her glare. "Of course not. This was my idea to expose Ludis."

"And what happens to you?"

"I don't know. I've pissed off a lot of people."

"People don't serve time for pissing someone off."

"Yeah, in this case, that's exactly what's going to happen."

Tears swam in her eyes and spilled over on her cheeks. "But you're a father. Anna needs you ... I need you."

Adam took in a deep breath and looked away. "Jared and Jennie will have custody of Anna. I hope you will still be part of her life."

A hard fist hit him in the chest, then another and another. Adam captured her hands, eased her back into his arms, and held her while she sobbed.

Chapter Twenty-Three

Pete's Diner, Sunday morning, four months later.

The small bell over the door of the diner dinged and Mary and Thomas McNeil strolled through the door. Calista dropped the pen on top of the sheet of paper on the counter and planted a smile on her face. As much as she had come to love the McNeils, sometimes it just hurt to be with them. A glance into Thomas's cobalt eyes could bring Calista to tears because she saw so much of Adam in him.

Before she could get out a hello, Adam's father wrapped her in a bear hug. "How are two of my favorite ladies doing?" he asked, releasing her and picking up Anna.

Anna wrapped both arms around her grandfather's neck and gave him a kiss on the cheek. "We're going to the zoo. I'm all ready."

"I thought you invited us to breakfast," Thomas said, sitting Anna back on her feet. He reached inside his back pocket and pulled out a folded piece of construction paper. "The zoo invitation mentioned breakfast."

Anna hugged Mary then pointed to the round table in the corner. "That is your table. Eat fast. The animals are out in the morning. If we don't hurry, they may all be taking a nap."

Pete's rough voice bellowed from the kitchen. "Keep your socks on, young lady," he said, opening the kitchen door. He balanced four plates in his hands. Setting two plates down next to Calista, he carried the others over to the table. He waited until Anna hugged Mary before lifting her onto the stool next to Calista. He handed her a fork. "Eat."

Calista took a moment to study Adam's family. Anna took two bites of her breakfast, bounced off the stool, and helped Pete hand out glasses of orange juice around the table. She had been in high gear ever since she woke up. For a four-year-old, a trip to the zoo was a big deal.

Over the last several weeks, Jared, Jennie, and Calista had established a routine that seemed to work well for Anna. During the week, Anna lived with Jennie and Jared. Calista would pick her up from daycare on Friday and keep her until Sunday when *the family* would all get together for some kind of outing.

It had been more than four months since the night she watched Adam cuffed and placed in a F.B.I. vehicle. Calista forced herself to stop crying at a drop of a hat. Tears were just messy, burned the back of her throat, and didn't do a damn bit of good.

Calista found solace with Anna. She needed to be around Adam's daughter as much as Anna seemed to need her. While Anna accepted the changes in her life with the exuberance of a child, she still had moments where the loss of her parents just became too much. When Anna cried out for her mother, Calista held her close and spent a lot of time getting Anna to talk about Rina. It was important the child understood the love her mother felt for her still lived on in Anna's heart.

While Anna's life seemed to have settled into a nice routine, Calista's day to day was at a dead-stop stand still. She couldn't get out of her own way and it was Adam's fault. He was everywhere— the diner, the grocery store, in her home. Calista couldn't turn around without sensing him. He lived in her dreams, haunted her night with exotic images of their time together, driving her body crazy with need until she feared even falling asleep.

Her heart felt empty, a relentless ache beyond anything she ever felt before. How in the hell was she supposed to move on? It seemed so impossible.

But her time for dragging her feet was over. She had a decision to make. An opportunity of a lifetime fell in her lap and there was only a few hours left before she lost that too.

Several months ago, she sent in an audition tape and an application to teach at a small college outside of Chicago. The position would give her access to amazing performance opportunities as well as be a great teaching experience. At the same time that offer came in, one of the local high schools lost their orchestra director. The position needed to be filled and Calista could begin immediately.

The local position was perfect because she wouldn't have to leave Anna. The job in Chicago could give her a breath of fresh air, a new perspective, and the simplest solution for the rut she was in.

Whatever position she chose, the decision had to be made today. If she didn't notify the selection committee by six o'clock, they would offer the position to someone else.

Anna dropped her hand on Calista's knee, pulling her out of her haze. Again, she planted a smile on her face and glanced down at the little girl.

"Please come to the zoo with me, Calista." She lowered her voice to a whisper. "It won't be fun without you there."

"You have six adults at your beck and call. You're going to have a blast. I'll be here when you get back."

Anna climbed up onto the stool and studied Calista. Her eyes narrowed before she said, "You're using your fake smile again. If you come with us, you won't be so sad." She reached for the sheet of paper in front of Calista and pointed to the name at the top of one of the two columns.

"This is my name, Anna."

Calista nodded and tried to ease the paper from the child's hands. Anna held on tight. "And that is Grandpa Pete's name and Grandpa T, right?"

"That's right."

Anna raised her gaze to Calista. "It's a list."

Calista swallowed. "I have a problem to solve and it helps me figure out the answer by making a list." The last thing she wanted was for Anna to worry about her leaving until Calista made the decision.

"And that's Daddy's name on the other side," Anna said, using her finger to outline Adam's name. "Why is he all by himself?"

The question momentarily stumped Calista. How in the heck was she supposed to answer?

Even thinking the words brought tears to the back of Calista's eyes. Using the palm of her hand, she turned her face toward the window, and wiped her cheeks. Jared and Jennie's car just pulled into the parking space. Taking in a cleansing breath, she pulled herself together.

"Your aunt and uncle just drove up. Don't you think you should finish Grandpa Pete's elephant pancake? The zoo is a big place and you're going to need the energy for all that walking."

Anna took a small bite and stared at her while she chewed. After swallowing, she lifted the paper and again pointed to her father's name. "Why is daddy's name way over here by himself?"

"This list is all the wonderful family who live close by."

Anna studied the sheet of paper for a long time before she spoke. "So these are all the people you love."

Calista smiled. "That's right."

"Does that mean you don't love my daddy because he's not here anymore?"

"Anna …"

"I would like to know the answer to that question too," a deep voice murmured from behind Calista.

As Calista's heart plummeted to the pit of her stomach, Anna shot out off her stool into her father's arms.

"I knew you were coming home, I just knew it," Anna cried into Adam's shoulder.

Calista didn't turn around. In fact, she couldn't move. It was as if every muscle in her body stopped working. But she didn't have to turn to know that Adam wrapped his arms around his daughter's small body and held her as tightly as Anna held onto him.

Thomas and Mary stood from the booth. Thomas reached for Adam first, drawing him into a huge hug and kissing both his cheeks.

Jennie moved around the group, dropped into the stool next to Calista and shot her a huge smile.

"Surprise! We didn't know if all the paperwork would make it through the different channels so we didn't say anything." Jennie stopped talking and studied Calista. "Take a breath," she said, running a hand up and down Calista's back.

She took a deep breath, but the sob in her throat kept it from reaching her lungs.

Adam's hard frame drew close, the fabric of his sport coat brushing against the thin cotton of her t-shirt. Part of her screamed for his hands on her, but he kept them down at his side.

"Calista?"

A shiver sliced through her. Jennie reached for Anna's plate and placed it on the table behind them. She then approached Adam and held out her arms.

"Sweetie, why don't you finish your breakfast? Your dad needs a moment alone with Calista."

Anna placed both of her hands on her dad's face, drawing his attention back to her. "You're not leaving again, are you?"

Adam hugged Anna and said, "No, baby girl. I'm not leaving."

The answer seemed to satisfy Anna and she squirmed out of his arms. The McNeils all sat back down.

Calista could feel their eyes on her. In fact, the entire diner was staring. As Adam's warmth ignited every cell in her body, she remained immobile. For the first time in her life, she had no idea what to do.

"Aren't you going to even look at me?" he asked, his breath caressing the tender skin at her neck.

"No, I don't think so."

He let out a deep chuckle. "Why?"

"It's easier this way."

"Calista, please turn around."

"No. When do you leave again?"

He moved in closer and his voice grew rough. "I'm not leaving. I'm here to stay."

And I don't believe you screamed in her head as her gaze landed on his fisted hands at his side. His entire body trembled as his fingers turned almost white from the clenching fist. Adam was holding it together by a thin thread.

Four months ago, she would have drawn him into her arms and held him until he relaxed. In fact, she had dreamed of this moment a hundred times over the last few weeks. Of course in her dreams, she was wearing something incredibly sexy instead of a washed out t-shirt and there weren't twenty-five people watching her every move, or in this case, lack of movement.

"If you can't look at me, then answer Anna's question."

The tears building in her throat let loose and streamed silently down her cheek.

Damn man! He had no right to do this to her again.

Calista took the sheet of paper, and with care, folded it in half. She fought to stay calm as her finger traced over the fold. She didn't know how many times her finger ran back and forth across the sheet of paper before Adam placed his hand over hers.

"I know I have no right to ask, but I need your answer."

Calista sucked in a breath, closed her eyes, and said the first thing that came to mind. "You are such a dumbshit, Adam Blake. After everything we have been through, how could you not know the answer?"

The next instant, he swirled her around and lifted her into his arms. Calista wrapped her arms around his neck and held on as tightly as Anna had only moments earlier. Burying her face into his shoulder, his spicy scent surrounded her as the pent-up sobs took over. Adam cradled her head against his chest until the sobs slowed.

Grabbing a fistful of napkins from the dispenser, she eased back and dabbed her eyes. "What happened? How are you here?"

He brought his lips over her eyes and rained kisses down her cheek until he was only inches from her mouth. "They decided I was more valuable to them on the outside then behind bars." He gave Thomas McNeil a quick nod. "And some powerful people came to bat for me."

"I don't understand, Adam. How are you free and why in the hell didn't anyone tell me this was in the works," she said, glaring at Thomas and Jared.

"There were so many ways the deal could have gone to hell. I didn't want you to get your hopes up and end up being hurt again." He brushed his lips across her forehead. "I'm sorry."

Heat began to rise in Calista's cheeks. She tried to push the disquieting thoughts from her mind, but they erupted without warning. "What are you sorry for, Adam? Are you sorry you never mentioned to me that you could be placed in a cell next to Ludis?" She clinched her hands into a fist. "Or are you sorry for not having enough faith in me, not believing I had the strength to stand by you no matter what?" Calista covered her face with her hands and rested her head against his chest.

Don't cry again, God, please don't cry again.

"Which one is it? What are you sorry for?"

"All of it, Calista, and none of it."

"What is that supposed to mean?"

Adam cupped her head in his hands. He caressed her forehead with his lips then rested his head on hers. "I'm not sorry for the time we spent together. If all that crap didn't happen, you wouldn't be standing in my arms. I'm sure as hell not sorry that you wedged yourself so deep into my heart, I can't tell where I begin and you end. As for not trusting you or believing you would stand by me, that's bullshit." His gaze darted to his daughter and he lowered his voice, "That's crazy. You are the bravest person I have ever known. You went at Ludis with a damn twig." He lifted her chin so they were eye to eye. "And I trusted you with Anna, trusted you to love her and help her understand how much Rina loved her. I trust you to help me keep her mother alive in her heart." He brought his lips down for a quick, but tender kiss. When he broke the kiss, his eyes grew a deeper shade of blue. "Don't ever accuse me of not having faith in you. I have never believed in anyone like I believe in you."

He tucked a strand of hair behind her ear and let out a noisy sigh. "I didn't tell you about the possible arrest because I just couldn't get the words out. I didn't want to hurt you. I hurt Rina and I can't ever take that back, but I can be different this time." With his thumb, he swiped the tears off her cheek. "I never want to make you cry again."

Calista took in a cleansing breath and tried to calm her racing heart. So many questions plagued her, but one stood out. "What was so important on that damn tape?"

Adam tore his gaze away from her and stared out the window. "Does it really matter now?"

"Yes, after everything we went through, after what Ludis did ..."

"Right before Annija's death, my grandfather made the decision to go completely legit for his daughter. He sent her to a rival family baptism to broker a deal. He was no longer in the business, no longer a threat. Ludis stormed the celebration and killed almost everyone in the church. It was all recorded. Annija survived the massacre, believing her father set her up. She grabbed the camera and ran." Adam turned and faced Calista. "I think she was leaving her family for good and had nowhere else to go but to my parents. The disk was proof that Ludis orchestrated the whole thing on his own."

Calista brought her hands over her mouth. "Good God, why?"

"You know the answer, Calista." He removed her hands, bringing them to his lips. "It's over. Ludis will never hurt anyone again." He paused a moment then said, "What else is bothering you?"

"What deal?"

"I have agreed to work for them."

"Who are *them*?"

"The guys at Langley."

"More secrets?"

"Not to you, never again to you, Calista." He massaged the tender area behind her ears. "I'm going to oversee training field operatives in areas that I specialize. I have given up my passports, agreeing to stay stateside until they can trust me again."

"That's it? You have to stay here?"

Her mind raced trying to figure out what the hell was so wrong. It sounded perfect to her. "What are you not telling me? I hear this huge *but*."

Calista had no idea why she asked the question. Maybe she just wanted a little heads up. It really didn't matter what he said because she wasn't going to allow fear of the unknown to chase away Adam Blake. She could deal with anything with Adam at her side.

"It just means that if you had dreams of honeymooning in Paris or some other romantic European or Far Eastern location, it can't happen if you marry me. And that's what I want. I need you as my wife, my life partner because I'm so damn in love with you, Calista Martin. I took the deal not because I had to, but because there is nowhere else I want to be. I've kept my emotions hidden for so long that I just don't know how to express them, but I'm a fast learner. I will not stay clueless for long." He reached for the sugar jar on the counter and placed it in front of her. "In the meantime, you can keep this close."

Letting out a tearful laugh, Calista pushed the sugar jar out of reach and wrapped her arms around Adam's middle. The sadness that surrounded her the last several weeks drained away, filling her heart with such overwhelming happiness, she didn't know how she could possibly contain it.

Adam's heart beat steady and strong against her cheek as his warm hands traced a pattern up and down her spine. She slid her arms up over his neck and tangled her fingers into the thick curls that rested at his collar. Pulling his head down, she moved her lips over his, flicking her tongue along his lower lip. He sucked in a breath and took control.

The clinking sounds of plates, odors from bacon frying, and the familiar voices of a diner full of customers disappeared. At that moment, Adam was her world. While his mouth explored hers, taking everything she was so willing to give, he brought his arms around her waist, lifting her until there wasn't anything but a layer of clothing separating them.

Adam consumed her, marking her as his possession. If she ever had doubted how Adam felt about her, he had just burned those doubts into oblivion.

As much as Calista never wanted the moment to come to an end, a child's voice calling her name broke through and she reluctantly ended the kiss. Anna stood next to her, her hand tugging on Calista's arm.

Calista swallowed as she untangled her arms and body from around the child's father. Heat rushed into her cheeks, but she refused to glance at the stares from several adults who just got a front seat view of the one of the best make-out sessions she ever had.

One glance at Adam's expression and she knew it took every ounce of self-control not to burst out laughing at her. She shot him a quick glare and pinched the sensitive area at his waist. He was just too damn pleased with himself.

Clearing her throat, she glanced down at Anna. She didn't know what to say so she just stayed quiet. The four-year-old didn't wait long to let her know what was so important.

"Is Daddy done telling you he is sorry?"

Biting back a laugh, Calista nodded, her gaze meeting Adam's. If possible, he tightened his hold on her.

"Then is the problem that you had to fix over?"

"Yes, I guess it is." What a difference a few minutes could make.

Anna let out an exasperated sigh. "Then can we please leave?"

Adam lifted his daughter up into his arms and they both hugged her tight. The restaurant erupted into laughter. Instead of hiding her face in Adam's shoulder, she faced her friends and family. This time, the smile on her lips was a real, heart-beaming smile she felt in her toes.

Anna squirmed out of her father's hold and climbed onto the stool. "One thing first," she said, reaching for Calista's pen. She unfolded the sheet of paper and scratched out her father's name. In large, block letters, she wrote his name next to hers. When done, she set the pen back on the counter and glanced up at them. "That's better. We're all together now."

Adam pulled her back into his arms as he held Calista close. His tear-filled eyes scanned his family. "That's right, baby girl. We're all together," he said, taking Calista's mouth for one more scorching kiss, a promise for what was to come.

This time, the kiss was interrupted with the cling at the door. Calista broke off the kiss. Father Anthony stood with his hands on his hips. Adam stepped away and pulled his best friend into a hug.

The priest gave Calista a quick smile. "So when am I performing the vows? After what I just witnessed, I figured you don't want to wait long."

Before Calista could find her tongue, Adam slapped the priest on his back.

"Today, after the zoo, or tomorrow at the latest."

More from This Author
(From *In the Shadow of Evil* by Nancy C. Weeks)

Anne Arundel County, Maryland
June 2005

Damn it, Nick. This isn't the time to start ignoring me.
Jennie McKenzie loosened her grip on her cell phone and dialed her foster brother again from the passenger seat of the SUV. *Pick up. Pick up. God, please pick up.*

Nick didn't know it yet, but they were getting the hell away from Mendoza — today. And if Nick tried to talk her out of it, she would drag him out by his ear.

When the call went directly to voice mail, a gut-wrenching dread cramped her stomach, forcing acid into her throat. *Why wasn't he answering his damn phone?*

Her tension spiked when the vehicle slowed and stopped on the shoulder of the two-lane country road. Jennie tore her eyes away from the silent cell phone and glanced over at the man in the driver's seat.

Jared McNeil. Not one of Mendoza's thugs, but a cop, an undercover cop.

Her racing heart settled with a glance. The calming effect Jared had on her was crazy. Jennie didn't trust anyone except Nick. But somehow she trusted the man sitting next to her. She may be nothing but a silly teenager in his eyes, but hell, his dark brown, wavy hair, cobalt blue eyes, and smoking-hot body did something to her sixteen-year-old heart. And when those amazing eyes smiled at her, she felt it from the tip of her head to her toes — and everywhere in between.

Damn it, stay focused. You have to get out of this mess.

A low growl came from the back of Jared's throat. "Jennie, I need your decision." His hands fisted on the steeling wheel and the tiny muscle in his jaw pulsed. "I have no grounds to remove you from Mendoza's home. But since you're a minor, and we arrested the two men with you at the testing center, I can at least place you in protective custody until we contact your caseworker."

A pair of robins flew in front of the passenger window from the tall oaks lining the road. They momentarily perched on the hood of the SUV then dashed off to the other side of the lane. That simple display of carefree abandonment cut deep into Jennie. As her fingers dug into her palm, she let out a shaky breath and asked, "What about Nick? I can't leave without him."

"I tried to talk to him. He blew me off. By placing you in protective custody … "

"No. I won't go anywhere without Nick."

Jared's expression went from concerned to frigid. It was like a curtain dropped down, cutting off his emotions.

Jennie lowered her head, her gaze on her lap. "Nick isn't … he doesn't warm up to people well. But Jared, he's not Mendoza's lackey."

She glanced at him from the corners of her eyes. His jaw was clenched and the muscles in his arms and shoulders grew taut. When his gaze met hers, she winced. He couldn't hide how unhappy he was with her.

"Nick isn't just my foster brother. He's my best friend and has had my back since my parents died. I can't leave him with Mendoza. He'll turn Nick into a carbon copy of himself."

"Any replies to your call?" Jared raised his eyebrows and nodded to the phone.

"No, he isn't answering me."

When Nick turned eighteen last month, Mendoza had offered her foster brother a job with his organization, giving Nick a glimpse into a lifestyle he could only dream of. Her brother was with Mendoza now. She could sense it. And the more time Nick spent with *him,* the more he began to look, walk, and talk like the arrogant psycho. It frightened Jennie to the core.

"Maybe that's your answer. He wants to stay with Mendoza. You can't make Nick into something he's not, Jennie. He's been in the foster care program his whole life. That changes a person. He isn't like you."

Jennie studied the man next to her. "You don't mean that. That's not what is going on here." Something was off. If only she could talk to Nick ... or Father Michael. Her godfather was on a mission for the Vatican in a remote area of South America, and Jennie hadn't been able to reach him during the chaos and upheaval of the last four months.

Then a sudden thought struck her like an open-hand slap across the face. Her gaze darted to Jared. One look and she knew she was right. "Shit, you can't ... damn it, Jared. Not Nick! You can't use him to get to Mendoza. You can't ... "

"Jennie—"

"No. You can't use Nick like that. Leaving him behind — you would be turning him into what you believe he is." *And that would rip my heart in two.*

Jared shook his head and started the SUV. The turn-off to Mendoza's long driveway was less than a mile away. Once they pulled into the private road, Mendoza's cameras would pick them up, which left very little time for Jennie to change Jared's mind. The walls inside the cab felt like they were closing in on her and she struggled to breathe. She could feel the anger radiating off Jared, but she wouldn't back down.

"You spoke to your caseworker?" His voice was controlled — almost calculated.

"Yes. She's arranging for a place for us to stay."

Jared let out a noisy sigh, reached for the key in the ignition, and turned off the motor. He faced her. "Mendoza's obsessively protective of you. Why?"

It took a moment for Jennie's mind to form an answer. "I saved his life."

"It's more than that."

Jennie could only nod. She didn't have an answer. All she knew for sure was that her soon-to-be guardian was soulless. He watched her, studied her like a bug under a magnifying glass; he made her skin crawl. He wanted something from her. It wasn't sexual. There was something far more sinister than lust in Mendoza's eyes. His very presence caused her spirit to shrivel.

She couldn't face Jared. It was too hard to see the disappointment in his eyes. So instead, she faced the front window. "I don't know what you want me to tell you. I know nothing about Mendoza, never met him before that day in downtown Little Italy." She closed her eyes and inhaled a cleansing breath. When she opened them, she peeked at Jared who stared at the massive estate that could barely be seen through the trees. She cleared her throat and said, "He was choking and none of the men with him did anything to help. I think they wanted him dead. And I'm not sure I blame them."

Jennie's mind began to replay the crazed nightmare. That moment on the sidewalk when Elías Mendoza's brooding, dark eyes had held hers, the universe she knew shifted. There had been something familiar about him, but for some reason, his presence sucked the life right out of her. Paralyzed and breathless, she had been unable to move.

She watched Mendoza reach for his fork and swallow a bite of pasta. In a split second, his eyes widened and he darted from his chair, grabbing his throat. Nick had tugged at her arm, then jumped the concrete barrier separating the restaurant from the sidewalk, and tried the Heimlich maneuver. But for all his efforts, Nick couldn't dislodge the obstruction. His plea for her help had finally penetrated her dazed state and she joined Nick on the patio. She didn't have the strength to lift Mendoza, but she did have first aid training. She repositioned Nick's hands. After several abdominal thrusts, the large bite of shrimp broke free.

"Why didn't Mendoza just hand us a twenty and have us removed from his sight? We were nothing to him." Jennie let out a shaky breath. "He manipulated the foster care program so we could live with him." Her eyes met Jared's. "We were in his home that night. The system doesn't work that fast. None of it makes any sense."

"Last chance, Jennie," he murmured. "I turn down Mendoza's private drive ... "

"I'll never turn my back on Nick."

She shifted and faced the front window. Jared let out a string of obscenities that made Jennie cringe. He turned the ignition back on and drove the last quarter of a mile, turning left onto the narrow road. The vehicle's wheels crunched on the gravel of the circular driveway near the front entrance. Beyond the house, manicured lawns covered three acres extending into woodland.

She gazed out at the helicopter sitting on the heliport behind the pool and tennis court. She faced the man next to her. Jared was working undercover to take down Mendoza and planned to use Nick to help him. If she couldn't convince him to back off, he was going to get himself, and Nick, killed.

"I've known Elías Mendoza for four months. You don't know who you're dealing with."

"I know who Mendoza is, Jennie."

"I'm not some stupid kid. You're only what? Five years older than me?"

"Seven. So?"

Jennie tightened her hold on her fingers to keep from back-handing the handsome, stubborn cop.

"Mendoza is ... I sense what's inside him. He makes my skin crawl. You're crazy if you think you can fool someone like him. He will ... "

Fear clogged Jennie's throat. She pushed down the shiver that wracked her body. "And you want to use Nick — " She gulped in a deep breath and exhaled. "My mom would've called Mendoza the Devil."

"Then let me get you the hell away from here. Once you're inside, I can't protect you." He forced the words through clenched teeth. "Look, Nick knows what he's providing Mendoza. He's not innocent, but he's still a kid, a stupid kid." Jared rubbed the back of his neck. "I wanted to turn him, have him work with us. With his hacking skills, he's our best way into Mendoza's organization. But I get it, bad idea." He placed a hand on Jennie's fisted hands. "We'll find another avenue. I'll go in for him. You stay here. Hide on the floorboard."

"Nick won't leave with you." Her eyes met Jared's. "But he'll listen to me. He'll come just because I ask him to. I have to do this." Worried Jared would try to stop her, she opened the passenger door, grabbed her backpack at her feet, and raced up the steps of the red brick colonial. The soft fragrance from the begonias, lavender, and sweet peas blooming in the beds near the door assaulted her senses, causing her to slow.

How did such beauty thrive here?

Wrenching her mind away from the familiar scents, she burst through the front door, her heart pounding. The guard in the foyer stepped out of her path as she scurried passed him.

"Miss McKenzie, is there something wrong? Can I help you?" he asked, but Jennie ignored him and jogged up the curved staircase, her sneakers squeaking on the polished hardwood.

"Nick, where are you? Damn it, Nick. Answer me."

She hurried into her room and barely glanced at the thick, padded wall covering, lush carpet, or opulent furnishings. Like the rest of the house, it was a pretty shell, and it left her cold. She tugged her backpack off her shoulders. Opening the numerous drawers in the walk-in closet, she yanked out only the items she originally brought into the house. Everything Mendoza purchased was left untouched. She wanted nothing from him.

When she didn't find Nick in his room, she opened his closet door, and reached into his hiding place for a small box of odds and ends he'd saved over the years. Pulling a couple of his favorite T-shirts and jeans off their hangers, she stuffed everything in her pack.

After a quick check of the second floor, she headed back downstairs and ran into Mendoza's personal assistant.

"Where's Nick?"

He shrugged. "I don't know. Talk to Mendoza."

Elías Mendoza's private study was in the wing at the back of the house, so she ran to it. She shoved passed the guard and reached for the doorknob. He yanked her hand away, placing his body in front of the door.

"You have certain privileges on the estate, Miss McKenzie, but no one gets through this door without this." His hand held a black metal detector. Jennie stepped away and raised her arms. After the guard ran the security wand along her body, he allowed her to enter.

She stormed into the private domain that few entered.

"Where's Nick?"

The immaculately dressed man behind the mahogany desk didn't bother glancing at her. His fingers toyed with a gold pen while he spoke on the phone.

"We will be landing in five hours. I want my orders carried out. *No, nos entendemos? Bueno,*" he said before laying the handset on the desk. When his dark eyes met Jennie's, she stepped back. He wasn't a tall man, but his intense, sadistic personality spewed power.

"Rudeness doesn't become you, Jennifer Marie. You forget yourself."

His eyes bore into her, his facial features hard as stone. She had seen the look before, but never had it been aimed at her.

"I can't find Nick."

Mendoza leaned back in his chair, flipping the pen back and forth between his fingers. "So much concern for that mutt. As you can see, he isn't here." He scanned the study before bringing his eyes back to Jennie.

Jennie's fist tightened. If only Nick could see the contempt in his idol's eyes right now. "My brother isn't a mutt."

"He's no relation to you. Have you finished your packing? The plane to Mexico City leaves in an hour."

Jennie cleared her throat and tried not to stutter. "It's time for Nick and me to leave. I appreciate everything you have done for us, but we don't belong here."

"Is that so?"

She swallowed, keeping eye contact as her pulse beat between her ears. She was surprised the sound didn't echo against the walls. "We appreciate that you want to reward us for helping you, but there's no need." She shrugged. "We would have done the same for anyone. You don't need to saddle yourself with two teenagers when you're moving back to Mexico."

Mendoza studied her, his eyes traveling the length of her. "I'm your guardian, Jennifer Marie. Where I go, you go."

"Not yet. The official papers haven't been signed." Jennie glanced everywhere except at him. She knew he would read the contempt in her eyes.

"And how do you think you are going to accomplish your dreams of college living on the streets of Baltimore?" He clenched his hands together and rested them on the desk. The silence that followed was deafening. "My people are still trying to locate your godfather. What will he say when he finds out I allowed you to go back to living in an abandoned building like a city rat?"

Jennie glanced down at her feet, heat rising in her cheeks. "The building wasn't abandoned, just old." She wasn't a runaway. People loved her, cared for her. Her godfather would move heaven and earth for her. But the man in front of her saw only what he wanted to see.

"We're not going back to Baltimore. I contacted Mrs. Arnold, my foster care caseworker this morning during one of the breaks between SAT tests." Jennie fussed with her cotton skirt. "There was a big misunderstanding. Mr. Stephenson is fine. Nick only knocked him out. We thought … well he's alive and well."

She forced down a lump in her throat and shuddered at the memory of the last family she had been placed with. She could still feel Mr. Stephenson's hands on her body, pinching her breast, trying to force his tongue down her throat. The memory made her want to heave her breakfast muffin and coffee. And the way his body dropped to the floor, the horrid sight of blood staining the carpet after Nick slammed the base of a lamp over his head, still gave her nightmares.

"And your plan is to turn your back on all I can offer you for what? To live under the roof of a child molester?"

"No, of course not. Mrs. Arnold will find us another family until we finish high school next year."

She couldn't pull her eyes away from his. Contempt and scorn radiated from his pores. Jennie held her breath and stiffened her leg muscles to keep from fidgeting. When Mendoza finally spoke, his voice was laced with something Jennie had never heard before. *Hatred.*

"Jennifer Marie, who else did you speak to during your break?" He broke eye contact, his concentration fixed on the computer monitor on his desk.

My God, he hates me. Why am I here?

"No one."

"I don't believe you, *mi querida.*"

Jennie couldn't breathe. His eyes turned black, cold. The stench of revulsion filled the air.

He knows. God, he knows about Jared.

Mendoza eased back in his chair. "We haven't spent much time together during your stay. That's my fault. I thought you understood." His eyes met hers. "No one betrays me." He reached for the monitor on his desk and turned it toward Jennie. When she didn't break eye contact, he nodded to the monitor.

"Your actions have consequences." His voice was so calm, it chilled her to the bone.

Jennie didn't want to see what was on the monitor. Fear pierced her soul. *Oh, Nick. Where are you?*

Mendoza rose and moved beside her. His hands grabbed the sides of her head and forced her to face the monitor. The security camera overlooked a patch of lawn off the rear patio by the pool. Several of Mendoza's men circled a man with dark hair grown down below his shoulders. His T-shirt clung to his athletic body. It took only seconds for the horror to slam home.

"Nick? No, make them stop!"

Each man took a turn striking Nick, his face beaten almost beyond recognition. Blood streamed from his eyes, nose, and mouth. His knees buckled and he dropped to the ground. One of the men kicked him in the ribs.

Jennie began to tremble. She yanked out of Mendoza's hold and dashed to the French doors. Mendoza grabbed a fistful of her hair and heaved her up against him.

"This is what happens when you betray me, *mi querida*." He clamped hold of her elbow and dragged her through the French doors. Her feet stumbled on the stone slab of the patio, but he didn't slow his pace.

When he reached his men, Mendoza yanked her arms behind her and held her against him. Nick's bloodshot eyes bore into hers. He screamed out when another foot landed on his kidney.

"Make them stop. They'll kill him. God, please make them stop."

Mendoza took her face in his hands. "It's time for you to make a choice."

"What choice?" Jennie sobbed.

Mendoza twisted her in the direction of the pool. "Which man lives?"

Four men dragged another man toward them. It took every man to hold him. He fought like a caged animal. "Jared?" Jennie glared at Mendoza. "What have you done?"

The right side of Jared's face was turning a dark, blackish-blue color, and blood pooled at the corners of his mouth where his lip had been split open. His left forearm jutted out from his elbow with an unnatural tilt.

Mendoza gripped Jennie's jaw and forced her to meet his gaze. "Jennifer Marie, which man do you choose?"

"I don't understand. Let them both go. I'll do anything."

A loud crack echoed across the lawn. The eerie sound bounced off the trees and vibrated back at them. The next instant, a bullet pierced Jared in the right upper thigh. A wet stain of blood seeped through his trousers. His leg collapsed from under him and he stumbled. One of the men grabbed hold of his broken arm and heaved him back up. A roar full of pain escaped his lips.

Jennie's eyes darted toward the location of the shooter. All she saw were trees. She wrenched herself free of Mendoza's hold and dove in front of Jared, blocking his body with hers.

"You made your choice." Mendoza turned and raced toward the helicopter.

Men in police uniforms and FBI jackets charged the lawn, guns drawn. Mendoza's men froze before all hell broke out. A couple of men lifted their guns but were hit in the chest before they got off one shot. The rest dove for cover.

Jennie heard none of it. Her heartbeat drowned out all sound. Everything around her grew silent, still. All her focus was on Elías Mendoza as he stepped into the helicopter. He turned and their gazes held. Even though he was a good thirty yards away, she heard every word he spoke as if he stood right next to her.

"*Mi querida,* they live because I allow it. You live because I allow it. *Usted pretence a mí.* You belong to me. Only me."

Jennie couldn't move. For an instant, her nightmares collided with her reality.

You live because I allow it.

Six words — night after night, year after year. The dreams had begun right after the death of her parents six years ago. A faceless man hovered over her and those words echoed in her head until she jolted awake.

Oh God. How is Mendoza connected to Mom and Dad?

Jennie's hands went to her throat. She couldn't catch her breath. *Stop him, don't let him get away* screamed inside her head, but she couldn't move. Her feet felt like they were encased in cement. The doors slammed shut and the helicopter lifted into the air. The next instant, a bullet grazed her arm. Jared slammed her body to the ground as another shot sliced through the air inches from her head.

She searched for Nick. His eyes met hers. He struggled to his knees and stood.

"Nick, drop," Jennie screamed, but her warning was too late.

Time slowed.

The third bullet whizzed over Jennie's head and sliced into Nick's cotton shirt. In her mind's eye, she saw the slug tear through his skin, and then bone, until it perforated his heart.

"No!"

A sharp stabbing pain erupted from deep inside her. On her hands and knees, she crawled across the grass to Nick. She lifted his head in her arms and slammed her hand down hard on the hole in his chest. Warm blood pulsed against her palm and seeped through her fingers.

"God, don't leave me. Nick?" she cried, but nothing came from the eighteen-year-old boy in her arms. His lifeless eyes stared up at her. She dragged his shoulders into her arms and rocked him back and forth as she wiped the sweat, blood, and tears from his face.

"Jennie, he's gone. Get down. There's a sniper in the woods," Jared yelled, shielding her body with his.

"No. He can't … " The words clogged her throat. "He can't leave me."

She glanced down at her hand covering the wound. The blood no longer pulsed.

The childhood pact they had made to each other flashed into her mind. His silly handshakes, his laughter, the warmth in his dark brown eyes when a nightmare tore her out of a deep sleep — it was all gone, Nick was gone.

Jared placed his hand over hers. "Jennie, there's nothing you can do for him." His voice shuddered.

Her eyes met his before she broke contact and cradled Nick's head in her arms. "Mendoza killed Nick. He may not have pulled the trigger, but he ordered it. Why?" she sobbed.

"I don't know, but he won't get away with it." Jared gaze followed the helicopter as it flew out of sight. "I'll find him and he will pay."

Jennie heard the words but didn't respond. Nick was gone. For the first time in her life, she knew what it felt like to be completely alone.

In the mood for more Crimson Romance?
Check out *Blood Secrets* by Shay Lacy at *CrimsonRomance.com*.

Made in the USA
Lexington, KY
21 March 2015